BOOK ONE IN THE *DARKNESS* TRILOGY

THE

SHADOWS

REBECCA HAMBY

Rebecca Hamby
The Shadows Book one in The Darkness Trilogy
Copyright @ Rebecca Hamby 2020

Cover Design: Pink Elephant Designs
Interior Formatting: Pink Elephant Designs
Editor: Rosanna Chiofalo Aponte

Dedicated to

My incredible husband who gave me the courage to follow my dreams and support me every step of the way.
Also, to the person who hyped me up from the beginning.
Your words of encouragement meant more to me than you will ever know. You know who you are.

Thank you

PLAYLIST

Rise Above It – I Prevail

Night Rider – Masked Wolf

Comatose – Skillet

Savior – Rise Against

Polyamorous – Breaking Benjamin

Not Gonna Die - Skillet

PROLOGUE

The air is becoming cooler with each passing day. Fall is in the air with evidence of the oranges, yellows, and reds painting the leaves that still remain on the trees. Walking along the sidewalk, I'm still wearing my apron from work. It was a long and busy morning at the café. There remained a constant line out the door the entirety of my shift. The cooling of the air makes for an even more enjoyable cup of coffee as patrons grabbed their morning pick-me-up and headed off to work.

I enjoy the café; it's a means for income but also my way of clearing my mind with the constant hustle and bustle of making coffee, grinding the beans, steaming the milk, and creating the foam art. It's a way of allowing an escape from my mind and becoming engulfed in the endless routine of making the world their morning cup of get up and go.

Sipping my own coffee, I admire the smells, sounds, and architecture of my surroundings. I've been in London now for roughly six months, and I couldn't be more content with my new place of residence.

I've been in Europe since I was eighteen, moving from city to city, working small jobs to make ends meet, but I've found a love for London and plan to stay here awhile. Since moving to Europe from the US and escaping the life I never desire to return to, I finally feel a sense of peace, contentment, and tranquility. At the young age of twenty, I have been through more in my life than most would encounter in their lifetime. Hence why I escaped my life and family in Florida and decided to escape to Europe as soon as I could. I wanted a place far away from my parents, where they wouldn't even bother trying to find me.

Finishing my coffee, I chuck it into a waste bin on the side of the road and continue my way down the sidewalk to my current residence—a small hostel where

I'm renting one room until I can save enough for something better. But for now, all I need is that one room. Walking past one of the many alleys that line the shops along the market, I catch a glimpse out of the corner of my eye of a dark figure in my peripherals. I don't have time to turn my head and see, before a pair of strong arms wrap around my waist and hoist me into the air. I try to suck in a breath to scream, but a hand clasps over my mouth, hindering any noise from escaping me.

———

As I'm carried down the alley, I'm spun around. I see two masked men at the back of a van, holding the doors open. My heart starts pounding like an iron fist, trying to escape my chest. Thrashing and kicking, I try to escape the hold this person has on me. The sheer strength of this person tells me it has to be a man, and a large man at that. He doesn't falter as he carries me like a child down the alleyway, squeezing me so hard around my waist that I can hardly breathe. His hand over my mouth is equally as strong, as I try to yell and scream for anyone to help me. But there is no one.

Just as the man is about to throw me in the van, I jerk my head back, headbutting his face. This does the trick as he releases the hold he has on me, and I crash to the asphalt with a heavy thud. Pain instantly shoots through my hips, ass, and knees as my body meets the wet ground. Finally free, I stand, aiming to make a break for it. Before I can even take a step, my vision turns to black as a blow to the back of my head has me meeting the asphalt once again. There it is— my old friend, darkness, consuming me. My head hits the ground just as I black out.

CHAPTER 1

SLOAN

Eight of us, eight of us girls, have been taken and placed in this small-ass room with no windows and a padlock on the door. I swear this shit only happens in movies, but here I am. Not twenty-four hours ago, I was at my job, working as a barista in London, and now look at me, locked in a room full of hysterical girls, sobbing and slowly losing their minds, wondering how they will get out of this mess.

I should be scared, I should be, but if you've lived the kind of life I've lived for the past twenty years of my life, this would seem almost normal. I moved to Europe when I turned eighteen, wandering around, picking up small jobs here and there to make enough money to stay at the cheapest hostels.

I escaped my parents the soonest I could. I couldn't waste another year of my life under their roof. Between the constant fighting, beatings, and touchy-feely friends of theirs, I left on my eighteenth birthday and never looked back. I tried to run away many times before but was always brought back by the police.

When I was fifteen years old, I was sexually assaulted. My parents had a few people over at the house and my father's friend, Jerry, noticed me reading in my room. He then proceeded to invite himself into my room before turning and locking my door behind him. He was rough, aggressive, and smelt of bong water and cigarettes. When I told my parents, my father beat me and told me to stop telling lies. My mother watched as she slowly slipped into her drugged state and passed out on the couch. Both were violent, drug-abusing alcoholics who had no right raising a child. Living under their roof taught me to fight, to be a survivor.

After being assaulted by Jerry, I told myself that would never happen again. Whenever my parents had any company over, I would sneak out my window and climb the fire escape to the roof. That's where I would read and lose myself in the alternative reality of the characters and stories of the books I was devouring. I would sit up there for hours; many nights, I would fall asleep under the stars, wishing and dreaming of a different world. That roof is where I planned my escape from my parents.

Sitting in this room of girls roughly my age, some even looking a little young, I looked around to see if I could use anything as a weapon. It was only a matter of time before the people who took us would be back to do God knows what to us. One couch, dingy and smelling of cigarettes and garbage, looked as though it had been left out in the rain for years.

Beside the sofa was a small end table with nothing on top. In the corner of the room was a doorway, with no door attached, which lead to a small bathroom and sink—there was one roll of toilet paper and nothing else. The whole room had a dark shaggy carpet, which had seen better days, and the walls were a beige color with nothing hanging on them. The only light in the room was overhead, and it flickered on and off every so often.

There was nothing, utterly nothing I could use as a weapon except the end table, but even that was plastic and weighed practically nothing. Standing up off the floor where I was sitting, I grabbed the table and snapped off one of the legs. I then proceeded to stand behind the door and wait. One of the girls watching me came over to stand beside me.

"What are you going to do with that," the shorter girl asked, looking at me with shy, curious eyes. She had the usual British accent that I'd become used to hearing since moving to London around six months ago. I had located a job quickly here and soon found myself working at the coffee shop and staying at a community building, not three blocks from my work.

"I'm going to beat the shit out of whoever took us," I replied with annoyance in my tone. The girl just looked up at me with sadness in her eyes.

"They will kill you before you get the chance; I wouldn't if I were you." Her tone was soft and quivering as she wrapped her arms around herself. I furrowed my eyes at her.

"Well, I am certainly not going to stay here and let them do whatever the fuck they plan on doing to us," I said bitterly.

She shrugged her shoulders and proceeded to walk away. I scoffed as I watched her take a seat on the couch and pull her knees into her chest. I sure wasn't going down without a fight. An hour or so passed, and my head started to hurt where the guy who grabbed me after work hit me. What the fuck did he hit me with, a fucking bat

Like I said before, this shit only happens in movies. Like that one with Liam Neeson. The one where his daughter gets abducted, and like the badass he is, he starts hunting and killing everyone to get her back. Good ending and all, but unless you have a badass dad like Liam, this situation looked like it wouldn't have such a good ending.

I was just about to sit down, when I heard the door handle start jerking. Someone was unlocking the door. I held up my plastic table leg with both hands and got into my best fighter's stance. The handle turned slowly, and the door started to open. My heart was pounding with fear, wondering who this was, but I braced myself as I lifted the leg up higher, ready to swing. Just then, a beautiful dark-haired woman walked through the doorway. She was of average height, with loose curls in her long dark hair, and she was wearing a tight black pencil-shaped dress that stopped just below her knees. Her face was delicate, with high cheekbones and full lips. Her eyes were soft, and just as she shut the door behind her, her eyes met mine. Her lips curled up into a small smile.

"Put that down, girl; it will do you no good here. Trust me, just put it down." Her voice was soft and soothing, almost hypnotic. She had an accent as well but not one I was familiar with. I lowered my table leg and rested it at my side.

Most of the girls now were all huddled together, still crying but trying to comfort one another with hugs and soothing words. The woman, who looked maybe twenty-five, ushered us all to stand together. I didn't hesitate. I walked over to the group of girls, still clutching the table leg.

"My name is Serena. I will be for all intents and purposes your liaison here at Stone Fortress. Do not be frightened. You've been selected to be the face of this establishment, so see it as an honor. I will show and teach you how to behave and properly conduct yourself in the superiors' presence. It may seem a bit overwhelming right now. Once you've become acclimated with your new surroundings, I can assure you, your attitudes of this place will change for the better." Serena spoke with such grace and formality. Most of the girls had stopped crying and continued to wipe the tears from their cheeks.

"I will first be taking you to your rooms. Each

room will hold four girls and will allow you to shower and get comfortable in your beds before tomorrow." She clasped her hands together and gave a huge smile as if she were excited for whatever the hell tomorrow had in store for us.

Each of the girls shook their heads in agreeance as I stood there in total shock at their cooperation.

"Uhm, excuse me, but what the fuck is happening tomorrow, and where the hell are we? You're acting as if we had a choice to be here; I was fucking kidnapped and smashed over the head with, well, I don't know what. I'm not honored to be here and would like to personally say fuck off and get me the hell out of here!" I yelled as I got in Serena's face. Just then, the door opened, and a massive, burly man came up to me and punched me square in the gut. I fell back, wrapping my arms around myself as I tried to get air back into my lungs. What the fuck? I heard Serena let out a small chuckle, that bitch. The other girls just stepped aside and left me lying on the floor as I gasped for air.

"What the fuck, you moron," I spat out, probably not the smartest thing to say, but oh well. Another equally large man came in, and both proceeded to grab me by the arms and hoist me to my feet.

"Now, ladies, your time here at Stone Fortress will be so much more enjoyable if you just cooperate. Don't be like this one here." Serena gestured over to me as I stood limply in both men's grasps. "You will be taken care of here and bathed in praises and treated like the beautiful women you are, so long as you obey the rules. Now please follow me, and I will escort you to your rooms," she turned on her heels, and like the good little girls they were, the rest of the girls followed behind her in a single file line. Not me, the fuck with that. I would show them why it was a mistake to take me. I started kicking and pulling my arms as hard as I could away from caveman one and caveman two, but no matter how hard I fought, their hold on me was too much. I could feel their grasp getting tighter as they dragged me behind the others.

Serena escorted us down a long, dark hallway lined with lanterns mounted on the walls. It smelled like rock and mud with a chilly breeze that gave me goosebumps. Continuing to thrash in their arms, I must have just barely nicked the junk of the guy on my right because he let out a low groan and then, with frustration, punched me in the gut once more.

Fuck, that one hurt. Gasping for air, I looked up to see the girls in front of me had stopped walking. Serena indicated to the first four girls to go ahead in the room on the left. Serena stood in the doorway, ushering the girls in before telling them to be ready for dinner in two hours. She then closed the door and locked it with a large iron key. Serena proceeded to walk another five steps and opened a door on her right. She ushered the last of us girls into this room, saying the same thing about being ready for dinner in two hours. The men practically threw my ass in the room, where I landed in a heap on the floor.

"Now, darling, I hope you can pull yourself together soon. I would hate to lose such a pretty girl because she is too strong-willed just to play the game the way it's intended. Just know, sweetheart, it's this or death, so choose wisely." With that, she closed the door, and the sound of iron clicking against iron indicated we were now locked in another room. For fucks sake.

CHAPTER 2

SLOAN

This new room was more prominent than the last room. Two sets of bunk beds lay side by side. They were freshly made, and deep purple comforters, sheets, and one pillow were on top of each. There were matching wardrobes in the far corner, and at the opposite side of the room, there was a door that led to a small bathroom. The bathroom had a vanity and a large oval mirror. The tile was sterile white, and the shower, hidden behind that blurry-looking glass, was just big enough for one person. The girls stuck to themselves with little conversation between us. The feeling of anxiety and dread filled the room with the anticipation of dinner. What should we expect? And what did we have to wear?

I was still in my barista uniform, consisting of black slacks and a long-sleeve button-up shirt. My shirt was covered in dirt marks all over the back and front, from being manhandled and thrown into the back of the van.

Walking to the wardrobes, I opened the double doors to see four long black dresses hanging neatly together. On the floor lay four pairs of shiny black heels that buckled at the ankle. What the fuck? I looked at the girls, who were watching me as I turned to the side to show them the contents of the wardrobe. All three girls made their way over to me and looked, one by one, through the four identical dresses.

"This one is my size," The smallest girl out of the four of us said as she lowered herself to examine the pairs of shoes.

"And these shoes are my size too. Do you think they want us to wear these to dinner?" the girl asked, her voice shaking.

The rest of the girls looked through the dresses, and we quickly realized each of us had our very own dress with matching shoes. Coincidence? I highly doubted it. Looking between the girls, my eyebrows raised, I asked, "Who wants to shower first?" No one said anything. "Fine, I will first." I sighed, genuinely wanting to be the first one. I felt so gross and disgusting just being in the first room and ending up on the dirty floor after being punched. I was all for taking the first shower.

"My name's Jules," the small girl said with a quivering voice. "What are your names?"

"Nastia," the tallest girl said first, brushing her short blonde hair behind her ears.

"Ann-Maria," the girl closest to my height, maybe five foot four, said as she looked toward me.

"Sloan," I said, looking over my shoulder before continuing to the bathroom to turn on the shower.

Surprisingly, the shower had warm water and was fully stocked with a floral-scented shampoo, conditioner, and a fresh soap bar. I found a stack of four white towels underneath the vanity, so I placed one on the rack closest to the shower before getting in. I made my shower quick, knowing there were three other girls needing one as well. After getting out of the shower, I wrapped myself up in my towel and made my way back to the bedroom. It looked as though the girls had already staked their claim to the beds. Thankfully there was a bottom bunk open. Jules, who was sitting on the top bed above mine, jumped down.

"I figured you might want the bottom bunk since I am way shorter than you." She couldn't even look me in the eye as she spoke. She was easily the most timid girl I had ever met.

"Thanks, Jules." I put my hand on her shoulder, showing her, she could trust me. We needed to band together if we wanted to make it out of this place.

The girls each took their showers, and we started getting ready, wearing the dresses chosen for us. I also discovered a tray of makeup, hairdryer, and curling iron in the bathroom vanity. To say I was surprised was an understatement. I chose to dry my hair, as did the rest of the girls, and I only put a coat of mascara on. I rarely wore makeup anyway, so the mascara would do. We all dressed and got ready for dinner. We sat on our beds and waited in silence. Waited for what exactly?

After about twenty minutes, we heard the familiar iron clanking of the door unlocking. The girl's breathing increased as the door swung open A tall gentleman in an all-black suit stood there. He didn't enter the room; however, he said, "Come with me, ladies," his voice deep and raspy. He was so tall that he barely fit in the doorway. The four of us stood from our beds and joined the other four girls standing behind the mystery man. I was the last to exit the room, allowing the other girls to walk in front of me. Turning to look the opposite way down the hall, I almost bumped my face right into the chest of the man who had punched me earlier today.

"Going somewhere, firecracker?" the massive man asked, looking down at me with a sly smile on his face. Shit.

"Just making sure my date is here to escort me to dinner," I said sarcastically. The asshole shoved me toward the back of the line without a response.

I followed the line of girls down the dark hallway and up a flight of stone stairs that ascended into a circle. I counted twenty-two stairs, and the closer we got to the top, the brighter the light was getting. As we turned out of the staircase, the room opened into an immaculate grand room, lit by a giant crystal chandelier. The floor was a sandy-gold marble color that made our heels echo with each footstep. The walls displayed magnificent oil paintings, which were full of colors. I wanted to stop and admire them; however, caveman one behind us saw me slacking in the rear and gave me a shove forward.

"Hands to yourself, asshole," I whispered behind me, but my little comment just made him shove me even harder. This motherfucker was testing my patience. Walking from the grand room, we entered through an archway that led to an even larger area. This room was definitely the dining room. In the center a large rectangular table stood with chairs lining each side. The chairs had that red velvet fabric that reminded me of royalty. Each seat was assembled with plates, crystal glasses, and a million utensils. Why one person needed five forks for one meal always confused me.

"Ladies, you all look magnificent," Serena complimented us as she stood from her chair, which was to the right of the head of the table. "You will find your names on the place cards at the seat where you will be dining. Please find yours promptly and stand behind your chair. Our host will be joining us momentarily," Serena ushered us to our chairs with her charming smile, displaying her bright white teeth.

Three girls had chairs on Serena's side, and the remaining five of us sat on the opposite side. I was the last chair opposite Serena, so I was the furthest away from the head of the table. Thank goodness for that. As we all made our way behind our chairs, Serena followed and stood behind her chair as well. Looking around at the dining room, I couldn't help but be fascinated by how gorgeous this place was. It had a very castle-like feel to it, with the paintings of random older people and beautiful landscapes. This place was so grand it oozed power and wealth. I continued taking it all in—one picture, one crystal chandelier at a time.

"Eyes front, firecracker," a familiar gruff voice whispered in my ear, making me jump. It was Mr. Caveman himself, breathing hot breath in my ear and giving my neck a hard jerk to the front of the table. As he released my neck, a tall man walked in from underneath the arched doorway.

The man was dressed in an all-black suit with a cranberry undershirt tailored to fit his body perfectly. The buttons of his shirt were open just enough to see his dark chest hair. His onyx hair was slicked back, long on top and short on the sides. I noticed the faint artwork on his left hand, but I couldn't make out what it was. He walked slowly and methodically, looking at each one of us girls one by one. None of the other girls looked up to meet his gaze; no doubt scared after Mr. Caveman just shoved me again. I, however, was looking right at the mysterious man. His skin was a shade of tan that made his wrinkles show a little too prominently. If I had to guess, he was in his late forties, maybe early fifties. He was in great shape, from what I could see. His broad shoulders filled out his jacket, and his waist was slim.

His eyes finally made their way to mine. His eyes resembled caverns of endless darkness, two ebony almond shaped eyes half covered by hooded lids. His expression was cold, and his brows pinched together as he continued to stare at me. He was challenging me to see if I would look away, no doubt. But I have known assholes like him all my life, unbeknownst to him, and I wasn't giving him the satisfaction. He didn't scare me. His eyes were locked on mine as he made his way to the head of the table. Another gentleman came up behind him, pulling out his seat for him. He sat down, unbuttoning his jacket, and placed his arms on the armrests of his velvet chair.

"Ladies, please take your seats," Serena gestured to us. Each of the girls slowly pulled out their chairs and took their seat, not once looking up from the table. Cowards. On the other hand, I pulled my chair out, not breaking eye contact from the mystery man.

Clearing his throat, he sat up taller, and his gaze drifted from mine to the rest of the table. A deep feeling of satisfaction warmed my belly as a small smile spread over my lips.

"Ladies, my name is Osiris. I will make this quick. I am a very busy man. You will be attending a party that I am hosting tomorrow night. You will do every-thing Serena tells you to do, for your future depends on it. Any nonsense, tricks, or attempts to escape, one of my men will shoot you. No questions. You are no longer the women you were yesterday. You are now employees of the Stone Fortress for the time being.

Your role and performance tomorrow will dictate your future and how your life will be moving forward. I would highly suggest you listen closely to Serena and behave like the ladies I know you can be."

Osiris then looked right into my eyes as he continued. "Any rude or challenging behavior may attract the type of people that can make your life, let's say, less than appealing. So, the choice is yours how you want to live out the rest of your time here. Enjoy this dinner, ladies, and I look forward to seeing you all tomorrow."

Osiris stood from his chair, buttoned up his jacket, and disappeared underneath the arched doorway. Holy fuck, what was that? The tension and fear that filled the room after his departure were so thick that I could have cut it with the many table knives displayed in front of me. Serena let out a loud clap, and several servants came out of the far doorway of the dining room, carrying trays of food. Each one placed food on our plates, which smelled amazing. My stomach let out a low growl. I didn't realize how ravenous I was until the smells started invading my nose. We all waited, not knowing if we were supposed to start eating, when Serena finally noticed.

"My goodness, girls, start eating; you must be starving," Serena said in a very sympathetic voice. Well, no shit, lady. I grabbed my utensils and dug into my plate. Serena took this time to explain the festivities' that would be occurring tomorrow.

"Now, ladies, Osiris is right. Tomorrow is a

momentous day for you all. You will be dressed to impress some of the most powerful and authoritative men from England, Amsterdam, Italy, Belgium, France, and Germany. All are coming to see you eight ladies personally. Your job tomorrow, and your only job, is to mingle and communicate with these men throughout the evening. Some may ask you to speak in private. I will say this only once, her eyes darting to mine. If and when they ask any of you to speak in private, you will do so. If you value your life, I would suggest no behavior that is unpleasant in any way. Each of you has a bullet with your name on it. It's up to you whether somebody will use those bullets," her tone was cold and emotionless. As much as I didn't want to admit it, she provoked chills trailing down my spine.

Looking through the girls, I noticed Jules, who was sitting beside me and on the verge of tears. Her eyes were swelling with the most extensive crocodile tears. Now, I have never been an expressive, emotional person, but Jules reminded me of an adolescent, her tiny frame and baby-like facial expressions. I couldn't imagine her being a day over sixteen or seventeen. I reached under the table and held her hand. She must've appreciated the gesture because her grip on my hand tightened. One single tear slid down her cheek, but she quickly wiped it away with her other hand.

The rest of the meal was silent. I mean, what the fuck are we supposed to talk about with anyone? Hey, my name is Sloane, and I was kidnapped after work and dragged into a van; how was your kidnapping? We finished eating, and the same gentlemen came in and removed our plates.

Serena cleared her throat and began again, "I suggest you ladies get a good night's sleep because tomorrow will be a late night for you. In addition to extra toiletries, fresh towels, and nightgowns, your outfits for tomorrow have been delivered to your rooms. Does anyone have any questions before you are released to your rooms for the night?" She looked around the table. I was shocked when I heard a voice speak up and ask,

"What happens after tomorrow night?" Nastia spoke, her words solid and unshaken.

"That will be decided by our guests tomorrow," Serena delivered with a sly ass grin stretching across her face. This statement only made me more confused; what did that even mean?

Just then, Caveman one and Caveman two came into the dining room and ushered us to follow them. Again, I made sure I was the last to follow the group; this allowed me to be more observant of my surroundings. Unfortunately, Mr. Caveman was right behind me, per usual. He was frequently pushing me and nudging me forward if I slowed down even the slightest. We made our way down the stairs again and down the long dark hallway. Our room was unlocked, and I followed Jules, Nastia, and Anna-Maria into our assigned room. Just as I crossed the threshold of the bedroom, I heard Mr. Caveman behind me.

"Have a good night, firecracker. I look forward to seeing someone try and tame you tomorrow." He left with a chuckle. Again, the sound of iron clashing against iron told me we were locked in. No one could tame me, fucker.

CHAPTER 3

SLOAN

When we entered our room, a neatly folded nightgown was placed on each of our beds, along with an assortment of toiletries, as promised by Serena. The nightgown was simple, just a plain T-shirt dress-like cover that hung just below my knees. We all undressed in silence and donned our gowns, slowly getting ready for bed. The silence was interrupted by Jules, who finally said what we were all thinking.

"They are selling us tomorrow, aren't they?" Her voice quivered.

It was clear that's what would happen. No one said anything. There was a long, drawn-out pause among us. Then Nastia spoke up.

"It would seem that way, yes." She didn't say it with sarcasm, but rather her tone suggested defeat. I have and will never be the person to admit any type of defeat, no matter how terrible the situation.

I have survived so much, and I refuse to accept this is where my story ends. I walked into the bathroom to brush my teeth and looked at myself for a long while in the giant oval mirror. My long blonde hair cascaded over my shoulders, and my liquid-blue eyes stared back at me. My lips were curled up in a scowl, and my eyebrows pinched together. My expression gave away not the slightest bit of fear, considering the circumstances.

Brushing my teeth, I didn't look away from the mirror, giving myself a mental pep talk for whatever tomorrow had in store for us. I heard someone walk up beside me. Turning, I saw Nastia standing beside me, also holding her toothbrush.

"Are you not scared of what might happen tomorrow?" Her tone was flat. She stared at me, waiting for my response. Washing my mouth out with water, I looked at her somber expression in the mirror.

"I will never show anyone my fear. I will never give anyone that satisfaction," my tone was even and firm.

"You sound American. Where did Osiris get you from?"

I turned to her before answering. "I'm originally from Florida, in the US. I moved to Europe when I was eighteen and have been on my own since." I usually never gave away any personal information about myself, but something about Nastia had me spilling more than I usually would. She was curious about me and slightly timid when talking. She nodded in understanding, and it had me thinking about her story.

"What about you? Where did they get you from?" I pulled my hair into a low ponytail. She looked at the floor for a second before lifting her head and locking eyes with mine.

"My father sold me to Osiris. I was in my room, and next thing I knew, I heard my mother crying from the living room. All of a sudden, my door slammed open. Two men came in and grabbed me, my father following behind them. He told me there was nothing he could do and to just go with them without fighting. I screamed for my mother, but she didn't even come. She just yelled out to me it was my father's fault. I arrived here moments before they threw you in the room." She was frowning, obviously sad, but had no tears in her eyes as she revealed her father's betrayal.

"My family used to be powerful and very wealthy until my father started to develop too much debt that he couldn't pay. I was his bargaining chip to wipe out his debt and start over. His only daughter," she said with a sigh.

Nastia was strong, her strength comparable to mine. We both had fucked-up families, and there was nothing we could do about it. We were born into terrible situations. She stood tall as she spoke about her family, and I admired her courage. Not knowing what to say to help comfort her, I just rested my hand on her shoulder,

"We can't give up on ourselves; that's what they want." Before I could walk past her to my assigned bed, she grabbed me in a tight embrace. Her arms closed around my shoulders, and I could sense her fear of what may happen to us all. I am no hugger, but she needed this. She needed my strength at that moment, so to assure her she wasn't alone in this, I hugged her back.

"Stay strong, Nastia. You are strong," I whispered in her ear low enough for only her and me to hear.

Lying in my assigned bed, I stared up at the metal frame above me—unable to sleep, because who would be able to sleep after that lovely family dinner we had? Jules tossed and turned above me, making the bed frame squeak with every movement. I rolled to my side and met Nastia's eyes staring back at me. Her eyes were puffy, and I could tell she had been holding back her tears long enough. She finally decided to cry them out. We just stared at each other for a long while, silently comforting one another as time slowly ticked away. Wiping her eyes, she adjusted her arm, resting her head in her palm.

"You're going to try and escape, aren't you?" Her voice was barely a whisper so that the other girls wouldn't hear. I was getting seriously impressed with how well this girl could read my thoughts, for only knowing me a day. I lifted my head as well and looked right into her eyes.

"You know it," I replied with determination threaded in my voice. Nastia gave me a slight smile.

"I want in." We both smiled at each other, and I gave her a slight nod. She rolled over to her other side and slowly drifted off to sleep. I lay on my back, pulling the covers to my neck, and started devising a plan that would hopefully get Nastia and me out of the Stone Fortress.

CHAPTER 4

SLOAN

A loud clang of iron woke me as our bedroom door swung open, banging into the wall. Sitting straight up, I wiped the sleep from my eyes quickly so that I could see who the intruder was. Standing in the doorway was my new best friend, Mr. Caveman.

"What in the actual hell?" I said. My voice still sounded groggy from sleep. Serena came in behind him, strolling over to our beds, looking elegant and refreshed from a perfect night's sleep. Bitch.

"Good morning, ladies. Wakey, wakey. We will be having breakfast within the next thirty minutes, so I suggest you get up and start getting ready." Her hands gestured over to the wardrobes as she spoke. "Please dress in the white attire that's been placed in your wardrobe, and Van will be here, waiting to escort you to the dining room. Chop, chop, I don't like to be made waiting." She clapped her hands together as she spoke and soon exited the room, leaving Mr. Caveman—or Van as she called him—to wait for us to dress.

"Are you going to give us some privacy, or just stand there looking dumb as fuck," I addressed Van as he filled the doorway with his enormous frame. His hands folded across his chest. He just gave me a sly grin, and I knew he wasn't going anywhere.

The girls grabbed their attire and headed to the bathroom to change, but for some reason, I was feeling extra feisty and decided to change right by my bed—right in full view of Van, who was scowling as he watched me dress. As I stripped off my pajamas and stood there in nothing but my panties, I saw Van's Adam's apple bob as he swallowed hard. I grabbed my dress and stepped into the fabric, not once losing eye contact with Van. My smile quickly pissed him off, and before I knew it, he had closed the gap between us in two long strides. Reaching his hand up, he gripped my neck, pulling me into his giant frame. His lips were right at my ear, and his warm breath gave me chills.

"Be careful, firecracker. You have no idea the kind of men that are waiting for you tonight. Keep acting like this, and I don't see you making it through dinner."

His words were an icy threat as I tried to wrap my head around what he was suggesting would happen tonight. He pushed me back just a little, so we were now face-to-face. I took a good look at his face. A scar across his right eyebrow was raised slightly, but the scar's edges were smooth; my guess is it happened with a very sharp blade. He's lucky he didn't lose his eye. He had a large tattoo that reached across the width of his neck, and it looked to be a tribal design. His eyes were a deep brown that looked almost black.

I didn't turn my face or drop my eye contact because that's not my style. I like to challenge men, and this piece of shit was no different. He pushed me backward, and I stumbled on my white-heeled shoes. He backed up toward the doorframe again and assumed the same position as before. Adjusting my dress, I looked over at the bathroom door and noticed the other girls had been watching intently, and I caught a slight smile curve up on Nastia's mouth. I shot her a wink, almost as if to say this will be fun.

We were escorted to the dining room once again, but this time I started to examine my surroundings with a lot more attention to detail. I looked for doorways, entrances, exits—anything that would allow an escape for Nastia and me. The grand room that we entered first after coming off the staircase had a massive double door entrance. It was arched, as most of the doorways were in this house, and had blurred glass, so you really couldn't see in or out, just faint shadows. To the left of the dining room was another large room with only a few pieces of furniture. From what I could see, it had a deep-red sofa and a couple of plush armchairs. Windows lined the room, bringing in a lot of natural lighting.

We entered the dining room, and to my surprise, Osiris and Serena were already sitting down in deep conversation. Serena's face looked troubled as she spoke in a low whisper. We crossed the archway, and Osiris waved off Serena. She stopped talking immediately as they both made eye contact with the eight of us.

"Ladies, please come in. Take your seats, and please help yourselves to breakfast," Serena waved her hand across the table that displayed a delicious spread of fresh fruit, bread, bacon, croissants, coffee, tea, and a spread of cheeses. None of us spoke as we took our seats and slowly started to reach for some food and drinks. I instantly went for the coffee; it had been too long for me not to have coffee. My usual consumption was greater than the average human. Taking a long gulp, I let out a sigh as I closed my eyes. When I opened them, I saw Osiris staring straight at me with an unreadable expression on his face. I took another sip, returning his glare.

"What is your name, girl?" he asked me with venom in his voice.

I wanted to say something like, shouldn't you know the girls' names you kidnap? Or even, fuck off. Instead, I simply answered, "Sloan," setting down my coffee mug and sitting back in my chair. He looked at me for a long while before saying anything.

"This is the one you were talking about, Serena?"

Serena looked away from me and back to Osiris. "Yes, sir, this is the one."

Why the fuck are they talking about me? I hated when people spoke about me as if I weren't there.

Osiris looked back at me with a Jack Nicholson-like smile and said, "I have a few friends that would love to meet with you tonight, Sloan." With a smile, he lifted his cup of coffee and took a small sip.

"I didn't realize I was so popular." My words dripped with all the sarcasm I could muster up. He let out a low chuckle before starting to stand and button one button on his jacket.

"I'm counting on it," he said, arching his brow in a dangerously seductive way.

Shit, Sloan, you are putting the biggest target on your back. Shut the fuck up. Why did I have to be so sarcastic? He left the room, brushing his hair back and leaving us to eat our breakfast. I looked to Serena and saw her glaring daggers at me.

"Now, Sloan, I hope you bring your best manners tonight; I would hate to see that fiery spirit ripped away from you at such a young age," she said as she continued staring at me.

"Ladies, since you are not aware of the importance of tonight, let me paint you the clearest picture." She cleared her throat. "Tonight, you will be on display to showcase your beauty to the highest bidder. Your beauty, charm, and elegance will surely be your ticket if you are hoping to be placed in a home that will treat you with respect, spoil you, and ensure that your future is one that most would only dream of. Attract the wrong bidder," she said coldly, "and I can promise you, death will be more pleasant—right in the middle of your sweet little heads." With that, she stood from her seat and clapped her hands once. Van and the other dipshit that escorted us here came in to escort us back to our rooms.

Serena was walking through the archway before she looked over her shoulder and said,

"I urge you all to look your absolute best tonight —shower, makeup, hair—and remember, you are in control of how you want your future to pan out." With a chuckle, she left the room.

Re-entering our rooms and listening to the door slam behind us, a furious Anna-Maria approached me. Her fingers poked my chest hard, "What the hell are you thinking, Sloan? You are making us all look bad with your sarcastic remarks and banter. Do you know where the fuck we are? What is about to happen to us all?" She was so angry that tears swelled in her eyes.

Pushing her off me, I retorted, "If it wasn't clear before, it sure as shit is now! They are selling us to rich old men who are going to do God knows what to us, and frankly, I would rather die than be some man's toy!" I yelled back at her. "So, if you are comfortable being bought by another human being, so be it. I'm sure as fuck not. I'm going to do every-thing I can to assure you I won't."

She backed away from me and stomped off to the bathroom. Jules sat on the edge of her bed with her arms wrapped around herself. She then got up and followed Anna-Maria into the toilet, like her faithful shadow. I walked to my bed and sprawled on my back across the tiny mattress. Nastia came and sat against the side of the bed. Her back to me.

"So, what's the plan?" She kept her voice low.

Thank God I have one competent person on my side. I sat up, propping myself on my elbows. "We wait for the best opportune moment and race for the nearest exit."

Yeah, it wasn't the best James Bond escape, but with the bit of information I had on the layout of this place, it was the best I had. We would have to improvise, be patient, and take the chance.

CHAPTER 5

SLOAN

The day flew by, no doubt from our fear. We all showered and dressed in the assigned attire. Tonight's required dress was an all-black dress with a slit up to our thigh on one side and the thinnest of spaghetti straps. They were so thin that I was genuinely afraid my boobs would bust one of the straps. I have a reasonably perky chest, and the cleavage was put on full display in this dress. My long blonde hair was curled just at the ends, making me look like a California girl with beach waves. My makeup was subtle, and I only put the smallest amount of liner, blending it into a wing. If I weren't in this particular situation, I would be wearing this exact outfit for a night out on the town. But here we were, dressing up to hopefully win the heart of the "nicer" bidders instead of the others.

Once we all finished, we anxiously sat on our beds waiting—waiting for God only knew what. My heart started to beat a little faster as I heard footsteps coming down the hallway. The door unlocked, and Van stood there with his usual look of anger plastered across his face.

"Come on," he grumbled as he turned his back to us, and we followed without any words. It was just us four, Anna-Maria, Jules, Nastia, and me, as we made our way down the long hallway and up the stairwell. Coming to the grand room, I was surprised to see servants everywhere, holding silver trays of bubbling champagne and hors d'oeuvres. There were men everywhere, dressed in black suits with either ties or bowties. They were talking among themselves and hadn't even noticed us.

My stomach ached, thinking about how one of these men might purchase me tonight. I swallowed hard in hopes that the bile threatening to come up would stay down. Van lead us to a small office style room at the opposite end of where the guests were. I saw the other girls had already been escorted inside. As soon as we got into the room, I turned my head and noticed a small hallway with French doors at the end, looking out to a garden of some sort. That would be my exit. That's how I was going to escape.

As soon as we were locked in the office room, I turned to Nastia. "There is a set of French doors down a long narrow hallway that lead to the outside, and I think that's our best bet," I whispered so no one else could hear. She gave me a sharp head nod in understanding, but before she could respond, Serena entered the room.

"Ladies, the time has come. Your job is to mingle, impress, and speak to as many guests as you can before the bidding commences. Remember, impress the right bidders, and your futures will be set from here. Impress the wrong, and well, you know the routine," she said with a bitchy grin. I wondered how Serena had gotten to this position? Had she been in our shoes at one point? Did Osiris buy her? Whatever, I didn't care. I needed to focus on our escape.

Serena left the room but came back reasonably quick, looking eager. "They're ready for you ladies now." She lifted her arm, gesturing for us to step through the doorway. We followed slowly, not wanting to join the guests so soon. I grabbed Nastia by the arm and tugged her close to me. If we were going to escape together, we would need to be close. Leaving the office, we followed Serena as she led us to the large front room that held the guests.

As we approached the room, all eyes were suddenly on us. Greedy, hungry eyes roamed over our bodies as if we were cattle at an auction. I couldn't hide my look of disgust as the middle-aged men drank us in, one by one.

Taking a glance around the room, I noticed no females whatsoever, strictly men. As we all stood in awkward silence in the doorway, I felt a shove from behind. Van's hand was on my lower back, pushing Nastia and me into the room. Looking over my shoulder, I saw his evil grin plastered on his face.

"Go on, firecracker. Your future awaits." Van's low, evil voice making the hair in the back of my neck rise.

Looking back to the room, I noticed some men had already started introducing themselves to some of the girls. Reaching out and shaking their hands, they pulled the girls in closer toward them as they exchanged smiles. I had no interest in introducing myself. All I wanted was to turn and make a break for the French doors. Now was not the time, though. Eyes were glued to us, making it impossible to sneak away just yet. I felt Nastia squeeze my arm as a young gentleman approached us.

"Ladies, you are absolutely breathtaking. Arno, Arno Griffin." He extended his hand to Nastia first. She politely accepted his hand.

"Nastia, sir," she responded with confidence. Arno looked Nastia up and down, not being discreet one bit. Fucking pig. Arno was roughly six foot two, with broad shoulders, black slicked-back hair, and a perfectly tailored suit with a white button up shirt and black tie. He had a five o'clock shadow that lightly dusted his jawline, and his smile was impeccable. Arno was no doubt very handsome, but knowing exactly why he was here with drew any attraction I had for him. His eyes were a deep hazel and gold color, and they stayed on Nastia for a long while until she looked away with a shy smile.

Arno then turned his attention to me, "And your name is?"

I, however, did not shake his hand; I simply looked at him with disgust before replying,

"Sloan." When he finally realized I was not going to shake his hand, he put both hands in his pocket and let out an amused chuckle.

"We have a wild one here, boys," he said over his shoulder while not taking his eyes off me. I hadn't noticed his clan of goons. They were coming up behind him with eager eyes running over Nastia and me. Both men were equally as tall as Arno, and both were wearing all-black suits as well. They looked identical, and then it hit me, they were twins. They were roughly six foot two, like Arno but maybe an inch taller, with shaggy black hair. One guy had his pulled in a bun, while the other had his styled with way too much gel.

"Ladies, these are my friends, Stefan and Jei," Arno indicated that Stefan, who was on his left, was the man with his hair in a bun. Jei, on his right, was the too much gel guy. I snorted a pathetic laugh before saying, "Charmed." I sported a less than pleasing half smile, causing the men to let out a deep laugh.

Stefan replied, "I like this one; she's spicy." He smiled and licked his bottom lip.

Then I put two and two together; these were the men we didn't want bidding on us. Oh well, my night wasn't going to get that far. I hoped. Tilting my head up to look at Stefan, since they were all so fucking tall, I sneered, "I don't think I am your flavor of spice." Grabbing Nastia by the arm, I tried to walk away, but a strong arm grabbed my wrist.

"Where do you think you're going, bitch?" Arno snarled as he squeezed my wrist a little too tight.

Trying to pull away from him but not being successful, I replied, "Bathroom. Don't worry, though, we'll be back." I shot Nastia a look, trying to telepathically tell her that was a fucking lie, and turned my attention back to Arno.

Letting my wrist go and giving me a death stare, he said, "Yes, you will." His tone was dangerous and full of threat.

I led Nastia back out to the hallway and turned to one of the wait staff. "Where are the restrooms?" My voice was calm and steady.

"Yes, it's down the hall to the left of the office." He pointed in the direction of the office. Perfect. That was close to our exit. I grabbed Nastia,

"This is it; we have to go now," I whispered, desperation in my voice.

Nastia looked utterly terrified, and I could feel her hesitation as she pulled her arm back from mine. "You go. I can't do this. I'm too scared," she admitted, not making eye contact with me.

Knowing I didn't have time to argue with her, I

lifted her chin. "Are you sure, Nastia? This life is the future you choose." Pointing to the room we just left, I watched her eyes follow my finger?

"I'm too scared, Sloan, I am not as brave as you. Just go, please. You're wasting time." She pushed me to go. "I will distract them as long as I can."

I gave her a quick hug and turned on my heels. Not looking back, I made my way to the hallway, where I saw the French doors. As I approached, I started to pray they were indeed unlocked. I hadn't thought about it until this moment. *Fucking idiot, Sloan.* To my surprise, the doors opened. Looking over my shoulder, I didn't see anyone following me. I slipped my body through the doorway and shut the door ever so quietly. I made it. I was outside.

The air was chilly as I took in a long breath of fresh air. Looking out into the night, I noticed there was a garden in front of me. Several stone pillars were lining the house, or rather, the fucking castle I was just in. No wonder it's called Stone Fortress. Bending down so I wouldn't be seen in the windows, I slowly made my way around the side of the house. Hoping I would find the driveway and exit without being spotted, I could feel my heart rate start to rise as fear began to swallow me.

I heard the sound of a door opening behind me and quickly pressed my back against the house so I wouldn't be seen. As the person stepped into view, I knew it was Van, and he looked infuriated. No doubt looking for me. I knelt a little more as he turned his line of sight away from me. As quickly as I could, I started running the opposite way. Just as I rounded the corner of the last stone pillar, my face collided with something hard, which made me stumble back.

"Well, well, what do we have here?"

CHAPTER 6

EVERETT

I felt her before I saw her. She was heaving and no doubt running from something or someone. She lifted her head after damn near running straight into my chest, and stared right into my eyes with an expression of total terror written all over her face. She was small, even in her obnoxiously tall heels. Her long blonde hair danced in the wind, and her eyes were hypnotizing as the moonlight beamed off their blue color. Her lips were quivering just slightly from the cold breeze. She was insanely gorgeous, just how I remembered her the last time I saw her.

Her eyes darted behind her as a man's voice yelled out, "Firecracker, where the hell do you think you're going?"

I recognized his voice before I even saw his face— Van. She looked terrified but also annoyed that he'd just referred to her as a firecracker. I chuckled inside but knew she was about to be in deep shit if he found her outside.

As soon as she turned back to me, I grabbed her face in my hands and kissed her with a force that would leave her lips bruised. She tried to push me off, but I grabbed the back of her neck and spun her around, so her body was pressing against the cold stone of the house. As I pinned her body to the wall, I released her face and whispered,

"Don't stop unless you want Van to shoot you for being out here, and frankly, that would be a waste." She looked at me, stunned, but I started to kiss her again before she could protest. To my surprise, she started kissing me back. Our tongues were fighting one another as I held her face with one hand and wrapped the other around her tiny waist.

Then I heard Van's footsteps come up behind us, and he cleared his throat. "Everett, I mean Mr. King, I didn't know you would be here tonight." He turned his attention to the girl I had pinned to the wall, my hand still holding on tight to her.

"What the fuck are you doing, firecracker? You're not supposed to be outside," he snarled, and just as he started reaching for her, I grabbed his arm, squeezing harder than necessary.

"I brought her out here with me, Van. I don't particularly like your private rooms. A little too stuffy for my liking; you know what I mean." I let his arm go, and he looked at me, stunned.

"Well, I have to insist she get back inside. Osiris

will not be happy if one of his girls is out here with no security." He tried to usher me back into the house.

Out of the shadows, my two closest friends appeared behind Van. "Ahh, who is this little sweetheart, Everett?" Colson asked as he took a swig from his beer. Van gave me another curious look.

"We'll be back in five." I gave him a head nod to tell him to fuck off, and he did so with no fuss. He knew who was really in charge around here, and it sure as hell wasn't Osiris. I let go of the girl and looked down at her.

"What is your name, love?" I asked as the three of us blocked her in with our bodies.

―――――

SLOAN

My back was flush against the freezing stone. I craned my neck up to see the three men who were now caging me in. Licking my bottom lip, I still felt the pressure of his kiss lingering, which made my brain fuzzy.

"Keep doing that, and I'm going to bite that lip, you understand?" Everett brushed my lips with his thumb.

I closed my eyes for a second longer than what would be considered normal and finally said, "Sloan." My voice was quivering, and goosebumps started to pebble my skin from the cold breeze. I opened my eyes. Everett looked down at me as he placed both hands in his pockets. His dark hair was shaved short on both sides, and the hair on top was a little longer. His eyes were a deep green as he narrowed them on me. He had a trim beard, and tattoos that climbed his neck up to the shaved spots on his head. He was in a black suit, as they all were, with the top buttons opened just slightly, exposing the ink decorating his chest. He looked to both of his friends, his grin full of mischief.

The guy on his right was around the same height as him, maybe six feet, tall as fuck. His long, shaggy blond hair was pulled back in a loose man bun, and small strands hung down, framing his face. His golden eyes were on me, and I noticed a tongue ring as he licked his lips in the most seductive way, making my core heat. He was the slimmest among them, as his suit hugged his body perfectly. He nodded at Everett and then turned his attention to the third man.

The third man was the tallest and biggest of the three. His vast shoulders were broad, and his hands overlapped each other in front of him, showing off his hand tattoos. His gray eyes were complex and unreadable, but I could see a glimmer of a nose piercing from the moonlight bouncing off his face. He looked pissed while he looked down at me, not trying to hide that he had been looking at my exposed thigh as the wind caught my dress and pulled it to the side. He also had tattoos around his neck, and I could see they extended down to his chest. His undershirt was unbuttoned a little more than Everett's, and I could see the chiseled edges of his chest muscles with the slightest bit of dark chest hair decorated across the peaks of his pecs. This man has never missed a day in the gym; that's for damn sure.

As all three men watched me intently, Everett finally broke the silence. "My name is Everett, but you know that already. This is Colson Cain." He gestured to the blond guy, and Colson shot me a wink. "And this is Dean Lawson." He nodded to the big guy, who just stood there with a fiery gaze.

"Sloan, is it? That's a very unusual name," Colson said as he took another swing of his beer. His accent was indeed British, but there was something different with his dialect. Something that was unmistakably noticeable compared to Everett's and Dean's thick accents.

"Yeah, well, I am not what people would call normal, I suppose." I wrapped my arms around my body, trying to shield the cold but having no luck.

"You know what they do to girls that run, don't you?" Everett asked, his eyes turning from mischief to danger in a millisecond. I looked away without answering. His gaze became more than I could handle.

"And if I stay here, I am as good as dead anyway, so why not go out in a blaze of glory?" I said with defeat etched in my voice. I'd been caught by three of the most handsome men I had ever seen. Internally I was hoping they would be my knights in shining armor here to rescue me from a fate worse than death. But I'd be a fool to think that any man at attendance was here to do anything but save me. We stood there just a moment longer, and I could feel the three of them eye-fucking me as I shivered. My nipples definitely were becoming peaks and no doubt visible through my sheer, skintight dress. Perfect.

Before long, Everett stepped closer and grabbed my arm, "Let's go, love, I have a bid to make." His voice was mischievous as he dragged me to Stone Fortress's front entrance.

"Hell yeah!" I heard Colson say behind us.

And just like that, I knew these were the men who would inevitably play a huge role in how tonight would end.

CHAPTER 7

SLOAN

With Everett holding tight to my forearm and either Dean or Colson's hand on my lower back—I wasn't sure which one—they led me back into Stone Fortress. Everett's touch was like a bolt of electricity coursing through my arm and body, or was it the hand on my lower back? The energy that surrounded these men had me feeling ... well, I don't know what. Everett had just saved me from Van, who would have been more than ready to kill me for my behavior. Yet this random stranger had been there for me, and he'd protected me from what would have been my ending.

Walking through the giant arched entranceway, we stood in the foyer where all the guests went quiet. Their eyes were suddenly on me, or at least I thought they were looking at me. The more I searched their faces, the more I noticed no one was actually looking at me at all. They were looking over the top of my head at the three men who had just escorted me inside.

I saw Nastia in the corner, surrounded by Arno and his crew. I started moving my way toward her, but a firm hand wrapped around the front of my throat, stopping me abruptly.

"You're staying with us," a low growl whispered in my ear, making me freeze. His touch was sending more shock waves throughout my skin and straight to my pussy. What the actual fuck was wrong with me? These men were here to purchase us, and a simple pet name turned me on. Isn't there a disease called Stockholm Syndrome where the captive becomes infatuated with her captors? His lips brushed my ear, sending chills through my body. I closed my eyes to his touch. Just then, a man approached us, and I opened my eyes to see Osiris standing in front of me. Clearing his throat, he looked down at me.

"Did you really think you could run from the Stone Fortress, Sloan?" His gaze was harsh, and his words made me want to punch him right in his smug face, the prick.

"Thank you, gentlemen, for bringing her back. I can assure you we have it taken care of from here. Please help yourselves to a drink and enjoy the rest of your evening. Sloan, if you will come with me now." Osiris reached out his hand, but before he could touch me, another hand grabbed his wrist, stopping him. Looking up, I saw Dean staring death at Osiris as his hand firmly squeezed Osiris's wrist. Osiris's face turned a shade of purple I didn't know was possible, while he yanked his hand free.

"Excuse Dean. We get rather possessive of what belongs to us," Everett said with his hand still wrapped around the front of my neck. "I believe there is a bidding tonight? We are ready to put in our offer if you wouldn't mind hurrying this along." There was a long pause between Everett and Osiris. I swallowed hard as my eyes drifted around the room and noticed every attendee watching this bitch fight that was taking place, and me being smack dab in the middle.

Osiris backed up and clapped his hands together, seemingly putting his best hostess face back on, but not before taking one last glance at me. "Gentlemen, I would like to start the bidding if we are all ready. Please gather around in the great room here, and ladies, please make your way to the front, next to Serena."

I thought Everett would let me join the other girls but he stood firm, not letting go of me even an inch. The other men noticed but didn't seem to challenge Everett, Colson, or Dean. They all just gathered closer and took their places as the rest of the girls lined up, side by side.

My heart was pounding as I looked at each girl, all of them looking utterly terrified, knowing they were about to be sold. I saw tears swell in Jules's eyes, and my heart wrenched for her. She was the youngest, trembling, but trying her hardest to appear strong. I looked over at Nastia, but she didn't meet my eyes.

Osiris called off the first girl's name, Flora, and started her bidding.

Two group of guys created a bidding war for her, but the winner was soon announced, and he stepped forward to claim his prize. He was an older man, maybe late forties, clean-cut, slightly overweight but not fat. His salt-and-pepper hair was the only thing that gave away his age; other than that, his face showed no visible wrinkles. He reached for her hand, and she accepted with no fuss.

The bidding continued going down the line. One by one, the girls were sold off as if they weren't human beings but objects. Bile rouse in my stomach, and I swallowed hard to keep it down. I didn't notice when I started to tremble until a rough hand started tracing shapes along my exposed back. My back muscles tensed as goosebumps prickled my skin. It was a small gesture, but it helped ease my trembles as I focused on what shapes he was making. I couldn't tell who it was but knew it must be one of the three. Were they trying to comfort me? I clenched my thighs together to stop the throbbing that had begun between my legs.

"Our last and final bid tonight … " a strong voice brought me back to reality. Osiris had his hand out, palm up, pointing right at me. "Is this beautiful young lady right here, Sloan." My name on his tongue sounded like it was hard for him to say, like venom stung his mouth just to say it. I held my breath as a voice came from the corner of the room.

"Here. I would like to put in the first bid."

I looked over and saw Arno with his hand slightly raised in the air, and a cruel smile splayed across his face. A deep growl vibrated behind me. Everett had his whole body pressed against mine, and he pulled me in tighter with his hand still around my neck.

"There will be no bidding. Whatever anyone bids, know that I will bid twice as high. Sloan will be coming with us. Her bid is closed." Everett's voice was stern, and I feared for anyone who challenged his threat. Just when I thought it was over, Arno made his way over to us and stood a little too close to me. He was looking right over my head, right at Everett.

"Now, you know the rules, Everett, why not make this a fair game, huh?" Arno said just loud enough for us to hear. The pause between the men was so long that I started to think no one was going to talk at all until a low chuckle sounded behind me.

"Arno, you forget your place, friend. I suggest you let this one go. No need to embarrass yourself in front of everyone here tonight," Colson said with an equally condescending tone that left Arno looking like his head may pop off from anger. I noticed Colson unbutton his jacket and push it back, placing his hands in his pockets. This little move was all the warning Arno needed, because right there on full display was a shoulder holster with two large handguns fitting perfectly inside, the handles standing in the ready position.

Arno glared daggers at Colson and his guns before

saying, "You boys have started a reputation for yourselves. You think because of who you are you're entitled to whatever the fuck you want. Well, don't forget who I am, Everett, and let this be your warning. Your time is coming. I'll be seeing you soon, firecracker." Arno winked at me before gesturing to his crew and walking out the arched doors and into the night.

"Congratulations, gentlemen, payment is expected immediately, and then you can be on your way. Thank you all again for coming, and I look forward to the next time," Osiris bellowed out loud as men began shuffling and congratulating one another.

I caught Nastia's eyes from across the room as she sat next to her buyer. She was frowning but gave me a tight nod. I didn't think I would ever see her again, and my stomach turned with the thought. I returned the nod before I was spun around, coming face to face with my buyer. Everett cupped my chin and tilted my head up toward his face, giving me a curious look.

"Let's go home; let me show you what it's like in our world." He turned and walked toward the door, with Dean and Colson stepping close behind us. Everett stepped aside, ushering me through first, giving me the lead. As soon as I stepped over the threshold of Stone Fortress, I turned to face the two men behind me. Colson, not hiding his excitement with a huge grin, and Dean still not showing any emotion, were right at my back. They reached for me, both offering their hand, but fear engulfed me, and I turned to run.

They were right there as if they knew I was going to try and escape. A colossal arm wrapped around my waist, lifting me off my feet. I started kicking my legs as hard as I could, but another pair of hands wrapped tightly around my legs.

"Get off of me! I belong to no one! I'm not something you can buy! Put me down, you motherfuckers!" I screamed, continuing to thrash even though I could hardly move. I heard Colson laughing and realized he was the one holding me immobile. Dean's arms around my waist were digging into my hip bones, making it hard to breathe. I continued to fight as much as possible, but I was quickly carried down the front steps. I shivered as the wind hit my exposed legs and back.

We started approaching a large, black Range Rover, and I knew if I was put in their vehicle, it would be over for me. I kicked and got one leg free, using all my strength, as my foot connected with Colson's jaw.

"Ahh, bloody hell!" he shouted as he dropped my other leg to hold his jaw. I took the opportunity and kicked again toward Dean and landed one hard kick behind us. I connected with something. Maybe his gut? He crumpled to the ground and started to cup his junk, and I internally laughed, knowing I just landed a pretty decent nut kick. I turned quickly, not knowing where I was going, but I knew I needed to run.

I made it to the driveway entrance, but I was

blocked by a pair of massive iron gates that were of course closed. Shaking the gates, I let out a groan just as a rigid body blanketed my back, pushing me painfully hard into the gates. His large frame was too much, and my already exhausted body was not able to escape him. He grabbed my arms, pulling them behind me and pushed them to my lower back. He rested his head on the side of my face. We were both panting from running, and I suddenly became painfully aware of how close his body was pushing against my back. I could feel his chest heaving and his warm breath against my cheek.

"Now, princess, if you want, you can go back to being their fucking prisoner and be sold off to the next filthy scumbag so he can do God knows what to your perfect little body, or you can come with us and let us save you from this shit show."

Did he say save me? I didn't have a response for him. When he started to grow impatient with my silence, he spun me around so that his body was now flush against my chest, and then he rested his forehead on mine.

"How do I know I can trust you?" I asked, genuinely wanting to know his answer.

He smiled before answering. "You don't. You'll just have to wait and see."

He was challenging me. As he pushed a piece of my hair behind my ear, his fingers brushed against my cheek. Closing my eyes, I remembered this man kissing me only thirty minutes ago to ensure I wouldn't be caught and undoubtedly killed.

My decision could be the worst decision of my life, or I could put my trust in these three strangers and allow them to be my escape from Stone Fortress. With that, I let out a sigh. "OK. I will come with you." I looked down at the ground, not seeing any other choice.

"Good choice. Now come on, you look like you're freezing." Everett grabbed my hand, and I willingly followed as we once again approached the Range Rover.

CHAPTER 8

SLOAN

Stepping into the Range Rover, I looked to the front and saw Dean in the driver's seat and Colson in the passenger seat. As soon as I opened the door, both men glared back at me, obviously mad that I had just assaulted them both. Colson's jaw was already starting to show a black-and-blue bruise, which would most likely swell. I smiled internally, secretly proud of myself for taking down two huge men who shouldn't have had any problem restraining someone my size.

Everett slid into the seat beside me and then instructed Dean to start driving. He adjusted his legs, spreading them wide enough to cover most of the back seat. I would never understand why all men felt the need to do that. He unbuttoned more of his shirt as he looked out the window. No one spoke, and the silence was starting to become too much. Colson reached over and turned on the radio. "Comatose" by Skillet was playing, and I sunk back down into my seat as I let the music fill my head. I scooted closer to my door, trying not to touch Everett's leg with my own.

Dean drove too fast for my liking, turning too sharply and pressing the gas beyond the legal limit. I clenched my seat belt, hoping we would get to our destination soon, when suddenly Dean turned so sharply that I slid across the back seat, my back falling into Everett's lap.

"I knew you would warm up to me, love." Everett looked down at me sprawled across his lap.

Shuffling forward, I let out a scoff, "Yeah, fucking right," I replied, making Colson laugh in the front seat.

"That's not what it looked like early tonight, sweetheart. You were fighting swords with your tongues from where I was standing," Colson joked, looking at me through the rearview mirror.

I just gave him a death stare, not having any retaliation; he was right. I did kiss him back, not entirely sure why other than I was scared to be caught. Why the fuck did I kiss him so willingly? That wasn't like me at all. *Ugh, Sloan, pull your shit together.*

I was silent the rest of the car ride, clutching the seat belt as tight as possible so I wouldn't go flying into Everett again. After about an hour of driving, we pulled up to another set of large black iron gates with a giant letter *K* in the middle. Dean rolled down his window and inserted a code on the keypad, and the doors slowly started to creak open. The driveway was more prolonged than Stone Fortress's driveway; I couldn't even see a house for a least a mile. When finally lights started to shine, and a massive, and I mean massive, mansion came into view. Instead of being stone like the dungeon I just came from, it was a modern white estate with black trim. An estate you would see in a magazine. It looked to be three stories, but it was in the middle of the night, so I couldn't entirely tell. There was a five-car garage off the side of the house that had black iron lanterns illuminating each door. My mouth was slightly ajar as I took in the view with such shock. I couldn't believe these three tatted-up gangsters lived here.

"If you keep your mouth open any longer, you might start to drool, princess," Everett blurted out, making me blush slightly.

I hadn't noticed how shocked my facial expression was until I looked up and saw that all three men were giving me sly smiles. Closing my mouth, I turned to look out the window again in hopes they would stop staring. Dean pulled up to the middle garage door and clicked a button on his visor that opened the door for us to enter.

"You guys live here?" I finally asked, which was no doubt a double question, but I asked anyway.

"You sound shocked," Dean replied as he carefully drove into the garage, clicking the button again to close the door behind us.

"I just wouldn't picture you three in a place like this." Yes, I admit, that was kind of a bitchy thing to say, but they genuinely didn't look like the men living in such a grand home, in my defense.

"Yeah, we live here. Believe it or not, we are kind of a big deal," Colson joked as he opened his door to exit the vehicle. He then came to my side and opened my door for me, reaching out his hand. I hesitated a moment but then decided to accept his hand as he helped me out of the back of the Range Rover.

Dean and Everett were already out of the car, making their way across the enormous garage full of expensive vehicles lined up one by one. I followed the two big guys as Colson trailed behind me. We walked up a short flight of stairs to a door that led into the most gorgeous house I had ever seen. Walking into a long hallway, I could see it opened up into a large oval entranceway with a double staircase leading to the second floor. I gaped as I continued to follow the guys through a large doorway that opened into the kitchen. It was stunning. All the marble was black with flakes of gold swirled through. The stainless-steel appliances matched one another, and the island was one of those infinity islands with marble extending to the floor. The kitchen featured a cozy sitting area that had a couch taking up the entire room. It was a deep charcoal-gray couch with throw pillows scattered all over it. The world's largest television was mounted on the wall above a fireplace, which Dean quickly ignited with a remote.

Dean and Colson made their way to the couch, jumping over the back and flipping on the Xbox console tucked away on a built-in shelf to the right of the television.

"How do you guys live here? I mean, I didn't mean it that way," I fumbled over my words, as Everett watched me in the doorway while he leaned against the counter.

"It's OK, Sloan, you meant it, but I guess I can punish you later." He gave me a smirk and took a long sip from a beer I hadn't noticed he grabbed. What the hell did he mean by that? My face turned red, and I couldn't hide the fury that bubbled up inside me, remembering this man had bought me only two hours ago.

"I can see the wheels in your head turning. Calm down. I'll show you the house and your room. You must be tired." Everett finished his beer and placed it in the sink before walking straight up to me. He was so close that I had to tilt my head up to his. Any other girl would probably have backed away, but my challenging attitude never wanted to back down. He stared down at me and brushed a loose strand of hair behind my ear. What was it about this gesture that made my skin shiver? It was seriously turning me on. Looking up at Everett, I thought he was going to say something else, but he just walked right past me.

"Come on, I'll show you your room," he said in a smooth tone, making butterflies erupt in my stomach. I looked over at Dean and Colson first, but they were already deep into a shooting game, with their focus glued on the television.

Turning, I followed Everett back through the entranceway and started up the stairs. Reaching the second floor, it split off to two long hallways, one off to the right and the other off to the left. Everett turned to the left and continued toward the very end. The hallway was lined with doors that were all closed, and my curiosity got the best of me.

"Are these rooms where you keep all the other girls you buy?" My smart-ass attitude couldn't help it. At that statement, Everett froze. Staring at his back, I could see he was taking a deep breath in from the way his broad shoulders rose and fell. Everett turned to face me, his gaze furious. Closing the gap between us with two long strides, he wrapped his hand around my neck. As he had done at Stone Fortress, he pushed me to the wall, pressing up against my body once more. His grip wasn't squeezing to the point where I couldn't breathe, but it was firm enough that I couldn't move my head, which was precisely what he wanted.

"I don't purchase girls, Sloan. Don't ever compare me to the filth that resides in Stone Fortress." His voice was low, anger pouring off him. I could feel his body heat on my chest as he placed his other hand against the wall beside me.

"Then why the fuck did you buy me?" I snarled. I didn't want him to think he scared me or had any power over me. He didn't speak for a moment, just looked down at me. His eyes ran up and down my body from my eyes to my chest and back up. He let out a low sigh and released me from his grip, but he was still pressing against my body and his hand remained on the wall.

"Because you don't belong in that world, Sloan. You're a lion who doesn't belong in a cage."

His words confused me. if I didn't belong in a cage, why did he purchase me?

"That's very confusing, considering the circumstance I'm currently in right now." I held his gaze. He didn't respond; he just turned and continued down the hallway.

Reaching a door at the end of the hallway, he opened it and ushered me inside. I stepped into a dark room and heard the flick of a light switch. Everett, right behind me, flicked on the lights, illuminating the room, and then my heart sank. I didn't realize I'd let out a small gasp as my eyes roamed the luxurious room. The walls were cream-white, and the bed was fit for a giant. The headboard extended to the ceiling; it was black with a diamond pattern that only rich people ever had. A black fireplace was placed at the corner of the room. Everett turned it on, pushing a button on a small remote. My eyes scanned the room, noticing a hideaway door that slid into the wall. The entrance led to a bathroom, which I could see only a portion of from where I stood. The black marble that was in the kitchen downstairs was also in the bathroom. Its gorgeous flakes of gold swirled through the black in a mesmerizing pattern.

"I'm noticing a theme here," I said, not turning around to look at Everett. I felt his warm breath on the back of my neck as he responded.

"And what theme is that, love?" his breath gave me chills as my body quivered from the warmness that was emanating from it. I turned my body toward him.

"It looks like a man decorated this house. Everything is so ... well, masculine."

"Well, the only people who live here, love, are three men. So, I would say it's rather fitting." His hands were in his pants pockets, and his head tilted to the side just slightly, as if he was confused by my question.

"What?" I asked, growing uncomfortable with his stare down.

"You don't seem afraid, despite all that has happened tonight. I'm trying to understand you, that's all."

He was right; any other girl would have lost their shit by now. Me on the other hand, my life had never been what people would say is normal. Every day was a surprise and a fight for survival. I guess my fear had been lost somewhere down the road. I had become a professional at hiding my emotions in their little black box in my head and hiding them deep down inside me.

"My life has always been full of fucked-up situations. This one is no different," I admitted with coldness in my voice. His gaze on me was full of, dare I say, sadness but mostly curiosity at what the hell I meant. I turned away from him, not being able to hold his eyes any longer. I didn't know how to act; I just knew I had to survive. That's what I was going to do now—survive.

CHAPTER 9

EVERETT

"This is a big fucking problem, Everett! We can't keep her here; she is in just as much danger being here as she was back at the Fortress," Dean scolded me in the kitchen after I left Sloan to rest in her room. His back was against the island with his arms folded tight against his chest. "You know, Osiris won't let that display of disrespect be swept under the fucking rug."

"I know, Dean, I know." I leaned back against the barstool and took a swig from my beer.

"You didn't see her when she ran out of the house. She was determined, Dean; she's a fighter. I couldn't just let her be shot for trying to escape. We've been there before, and we all fought to get out in our own fucking way. Or have you already forgotten? That was her escape, and I couldn't let her fail. She is different."

Rubbing my eyes with my hands, I heard Dean sigh as he made his way to the barstool next to me. "I remember it like it was yesterday, Everett." his voice was almost a whisper as he recollected the time we spent in Stone Fortress together as young boys.

It was different back then. Osiris wasn't in the business of sex trafficking, but instead he was in charge of training and teaching kids how to be the best mercenaries in Europe. He was part of a group called The Shadows. When we were twelve years old, we were sent to Stone Fortress. All three of us from powerful families our own agendas for our lives. My father and grandfather were also in The Shadows, so naturally this is what they wanted for me as well. A cold-blooded, heartless murderer trained to do the dirty work of others who were too big of pussies to do it themselves.

Dean escaped his brutal family and was found wandering the streets of Birmingham England, thieving and doing whatever he could to survive the harsh streets. The local police picked him up, but instead of sending him to an orphanage like most kids in that situation, he was brought to Osiris. Most of the PD was on Osiris's payroll, so whenever they found a physically fit young man who displayed potential, he was brought to the Stone Fortress.

Colson's story began when his father had started to accumulate debts throughout the gambling world. He was finally approached with an ultimatum—pay the debt off or die. He was not a man to admit defeat, so he offered a bargain. In exchange for his son, half his debt would be paid off. The man in charge of collecting his debt was none other than Osiris's father, Ezra. He knew he wanted Colson for the Shadows and didn't want his reputation altered by agreeing to another man's bargain. With that, he accepted Colson as a price but ended up killing Colson's father anyway.

You could say the three of us haven't been dealt the hand of a normal childhood. We were trained every day for the next six years in all aspects of becoming mercenaries, from hand-to-hand combat to long-range shooting, to poisoning and all the ways to kill a man in the most painful ways imaginable. We were bred to be nothing but killers. When we finished our training, we were instantly handed jobs, one after the other. From killing political party candidates to government officials who weren't fitting the script. We were the ones to make them disappear. The last seven years, we did exactly as we were told—no questions asked.

"I couldn't let them break her, Dean. She doesn't deserve the treatment she would have received. Imagine if Arno got his hands on her? She would be dead in the next three months."

"Yeah, I know, man, I know." Dean sighed.

I heard a faint rustling noise and turned around to see Colson sitting up on the couch, stretching as he let out a long yawn.

"What the fuck are you both arguing about now?"

he asked, standing up and coming over to lean his forearms on the counter. I looked up at Colson as he brushed his shaggy blond hair back with his hand.

"Nothing, just not sure what the fuck is going to happen now that Sloan is here," I admitted, not regretting my decision, but truly not knowing what kind of repercussion was going to come from our little stunt.

"What do you mean, now that I am here?" I heard her voice from the entrance of the kitchen. She was standing against the doorframe, with a long white T-shirt I let her borrow to sleep in, since I hadn't planned on bringing a girl back to the house. I gave myself a mental reminder to arrange for clothes to be brought over tomorrow. She looked tired, her hair was slightly teased, her sleepy blue eyes were barely able to stay open, and her lean bare legs crossed over one another. She was pure perfection in nothing but my white shirt.

"Am I safe here?" she asked, sounding concerned.

The guys and I looked back and forth at one another, not sure how to answer that question. Was she safe here? I mean, we were three of the best mercenaries in the world. Of course, she was safe with us.

"Anywhere we are, sweetheart, you're safe," Colson said with confidence as he stood up from resting his arms on the island.

"So why am I here then?"

"You should be getting some rest," I said.

"Well, it's kind of hard to rest, knowing I'm in a mansion with three random dudes who just purchased me earlier today. Still slightly confused why you did buy me." Her voice was full of sarcasm. She let out a yawn as she raised her arms above her head to stretch. Her shirt started rising even higher up her thigh, exposing more and more of her legs. My cock twitched in my jeans. Damn, what have I done, bringing her here? She walked over to us and placed her hands on the island.

"So, since we are all still awake, can I please have some coffee?" she pleaded.

"Sure can!" Colson said with a clap of his hands as he turned to start brewing a fresh cup of coffee.

Sloan looked from me to Dean before asking, "What are you both staring at?"

"Just curious as to why you're so comfortable having coffee with your three captors, that's all," Dean said, expressing my thoughts exactly.

She tilted her head a bit before responding. "It was either them or you, and at the moment, I couldn't see what would be fun about staying in that shithole of a prison. I guess I made the right choice, considering the house I'm currently standing in."

Colson let out a chuckle as he turned back toward us and sat a fresh cup of coffee in front of Sloan.

"Thank you, Jesus," Sloan said as she took a deep breath, inhaling the scent of fresh coffee.

"Not, Jesus, but close. Just call me Colson for now."

I pulled out the barstool next to me and gestured for her to take a seat. She did so, hugging her mug close to her chest. The room was quiet for a bit while Colson brought Dean and I coffee as well. She took a few sips of her coffee, savoring each taste as if it were giving her life.

"What's The Shadows?"

The three of us turned and gaped at her in confusion. Did she just overhear our whole conversation?

CHAPTER 10

DEAN

She fucking heard us! Now she knows who we are and what vile, god-awful shit we're bred to do. Before anyone could answer her, the whole house suddenly went dark. Someone had triggered our silent alarm system, shutting off the lights in the house. Moments later, dimly lit red lights started illuminating the inside of the house.

"What the fuck?" Sloan practically screamed out our location to whoever was trying to ambush us.

Luckily, Colson—being the fastest fucker I know—was by her in an instant, clapping his hand over her mouth before she could say another word.

"Take her to the safe room, lock her in, and meet us back in the security office," Everett whispered to Colson, careful not to give our position away to whoever was out there.

"Got it," Colson replied. Both of them disappeared

down the dark hallway leading to the entrance to our safe room. Everett and I grabbed our guns, which were still strapped to our holsters, and took off toward our security room on the other side of the house. We were careful, ducking around every window as quickly and quietly as we could. Killing was what we did, and it's what we were trained to do. Whoever just broke through our security was in for a rough night.

Making our way to the office, Everett flipped the switch under the desk that turned on all our monitors, displaying eight different camera feeds. Each camera was a live feed that recorded at all times. Glancing around to the monitors, I spotted two men in all-black clothing, heavily armed with what looked to be M4s.

"Right there, two men coming around the east side of the house, toward the pool house," I whispered to Everett.

He looked at the monitors and replied, "There seems to be two more on the south end as well."

"One guess, this is because she's here," I said with heavy sarcasm, looking over my shoulder to meet his gaze.

"I don't give a fuck why they are here; all I know is none of them are leaving here alive." Everett's tone was evil. There's the Everett I loved. He was one of the most dangerous men I knew, apart from myself and Colson. Everett killed first and asked questions later.

"Let's go have some fun," I said with a wicked smile on my face. Just then, Colson came running into the room, gun in hand. "How many?"

"Four. Looks like tonight just got a little more interesting." I grinned at Colson.

"All right then, let's go have some fun," Colson said as the three of us filed out of the office and split up, knowing exactly where each of us was going. Our team was more than a team; we had a way of knowing what the other was thinking. We grew up together, fought together, and created a stronger brotherhood than any other team The Shadows could have made. We were a force to be reckoned with, a powerhouse that had killed more targets than any other team. This one was no different. Whoever these people were, they were about to find out why we were the best. This was going to be the biggest mistake of their lives, and no doubt the last.

CHAPTER 11

SLOAN

Just as the red lights illuminated the corners of the house, I felt Colson's hand wrap around my mouth, prohibiting me from speaking any further. Before I was able to protest and fight off his hand, my body was being dragged down a long hallway I'd yet to explore. Colson's grip on my hand was firm and slightly painful. We were moving so quickly I could barely keep up with his long strides. I hadn't slept in what seemed like days, but at this moment, my heart and adrenaline were pumping at maximum speed. We stopped abruptly in front of a tall bookshelf, and I half expected him to pull on a book, revealing a hidden door. Instead, Colson placed his hand flat underneath the third shelf down. After about three seconds, I heard the latch of a door unlock and the bookshelf slid to the left, exposing a set of black stairs illuminated by tiny LED lights. They were just bright enough to show each stair.

Colson then started to pull me down the stairs at an equally fast pace as before. Reaching the bottom of the stairs, I saw a door at the end of a short hallway. It was cold, and the walls were stone. The only light in the hallway was an overhead light placed atop the door. We stopped in front of the door, there was a touchscreen pad located on the right side of the door. Colson placed his palm flat on the screen, which started to read his biometrics. Once finished, the door unlocked.

"OK, James Bond," I joked as he ushered me into the tiny room.

"This is our safe room. You'll be fine in here until we get back. Don't touch anything," Colson warned me before turning and rushing to the door.

"Wait, where are you going? What is going on?" I pleaded, needing some answers.

"We'll explain later. Just know you're safe here." Then he left, shutting the door behind him.

Racing over to the door, I tried the handle, but of course it was locked. These fuckers had a lot of explaining to do. Spinning around to examine this new room, I saw four computer monitors hanging on the wall. Listen, I know he said not to touch anything, but damn, my curiosity was getting the best of me. Finding a small remote on the table below the monitors, I clicked the power button, powering up all four monitors.

Each monitor looked to be a live recording of their property. Each one displayed a different angle. Looking at the monitors, I could see dark figures crouching down and moving along the house's walls. Each person was carrying a rifle and dressed in all black apparel. Were we being attacked? Who the fuck were these guys?

Following the men on each monitor, I counted four attackers. That's not the best odds—four against three—and these guys looked to be professionals. They were all strapped with gear and looked like the guys in the military first-person shooter games. I could hear my heart beating in my chest as my eyes followed the men around the house. Two men crouched down by a small building behind the house, and I guessed it might be the pool house. Waiting for them to move and do something, I caught sight of another figure creeping up behind them. Squinting to try and get a better glance at who this new person was, I let out a small scream as the man grabbed the attacker from behind and slit his throat with one fast slice. He then raised a gun and shot the second man in the back of the head. As the man turned away, I could see his face—Everett! Holy fucking shit! Fucking Everett just murdered two men.

Who the fuck were these guys? Everett disappeared off the monitor, running from the two dead men, now on the floor. Scanning the other monitors, I saw the other two attackers crouch lower after hearing the gunshot from Everett. They looked to be standing beside a large sliding glass door. I'd seen these doors earlier today in the room where Dean and Colson were playing video games. Maybe the living room? Staring intently at the monitors, both attackers reacted to something off-camera. Both men turned their heads behind them. Suddenly they both dropped dead, blood quickly pooling around their heads on the concrete.

Shaking now, I stared at the monitor as the pool of blood became larger and larger around their lifeless bodies. Just as I was about to turn off the monitors, I saw Dean and Colson walk into the frame, both holding rifles by their sides. Dean knelt beside one of the men and looked to be checking his pulse, or lack thereof. I had no doubt these men were both dead from the amount of blood encircling their bodies.

I had to get out of here. If these guys were willing to kill four men so quickly and without remorse, what were they going to do to me? I ran to the door of the room and tried the handle, jiggling it harder and harder. It was no use; I was locked in here, thanks to Colson. There was no other way out. No windows, no trap doors, no magical genie lamp that I could rub and wish myself out of here. I was fucked.

I paced the room for what felt like hours until I heard footsteps coming down the hallway. I raced to the door and stood on the opposite side, so it would conceal me when the door was opened. I heard the familiar sound of the door unlocking from one of their biometric handprints. The door swung open and squished me against the wall.

"What the fuck? Where is she, Colson?" Everett yelled as he stepped further into the room.

"The fuck should I know? I put her here and locked the door behind me."

"Perfect, now we have a scavenger hunt to deal with." Dean sighed as he, too, stepped into the room.

Once I felt positive they were all in the room, I pushed the door away from me and bolted out of the room. Not much of a plan, but I needed to try. I made it to the first step before a pair of giant hands wrapped around my waist, hoisting me off the ground.

"Put me down, you motherfucker!" I yelled as I kicked and thrashed in the arms of whoever had me. He spun me around, making his way back to the room. Looking up, I noticed Everett and Colson waiting for me patiently. That left Dean. Dean was the fucker carrying me. He dropped me to the ground in front of Everett, who was giving me a death glare.

"Where the hell do you think you're going, love?" he asked. Dean stood behind me, blocking my exit.

"Anywhere but here with you three murdering psychopaths."

OK, so that was probably not the best thing to say, considering I just watched the three of them kill four men.

"And you think you're safer out there when people are trying to kidnap or kill you?" This came from behind Everett, and I arched my head around his body to see Colson sitting on the edge of a chair, flipping through the monitors with the remote.

"Didn't I tell you not to touch anything?"

I looked away from Colson and back toward the monitors, which still displayed four dead bodies scattered around their home.

"Can you blame me?" I scoffed back. Everett rubbed his hands through his hair and turned away from me.

"Who were they?" My voice was barely above a whisper. I wasn't even sure if anyone had heard me from the long silence that filled the room.

"They were here for you, Sloan. They're hired mercenaries, like us, tasked with either killing you or kidnapping you again." Everett's back was to me the whole time he spoke.

I was beyond confused. Why would anyone try to kill or kidnap me, again? What had I ever done in my life to deserve this type of attention? I was a fucking barista not four days ago, working hard to earn my way in this beautiful country. I had no real friends other than my co-workers. I didn't do drugs and hardly drank, so I hadn't fallen into the wrong crowd. So why was this happening to me?

"Why me?" I had nothing else to say but why? Everett turned back to me, his face emotionless and relaxed, like he hadn't just killed two people. He closed the gap between us until we were so close that I was forced to crane my neck to look up at him. Fuck,

I hated being short. His blue eyes were reflecting the small amount of light that was coming from the room. Damn this man and his gorgeous face. He cupped my face, and I relaxed into his touch, closing my eyes. Even though I just witnessed this man murder someone, I felt oddly safe in his embrace. His warm hand heated my face as he rubbed his thumb along the side of my cheek.

"They came for you because we made a mistake, love. This is a punishment for our stupidity." I heard an annoyed chuckle come from behind me.

"Our stupidity, Everett? Try your stupidity. I told you this was fucked up from the beginning." Dean's tone was bitter and cold. "This little thing of wanting to protect her will only get her killed," Dean turned and left the three of us in the safe room. For a moment, all we heard were Dean's footsteps ascending the staircase, back through the secret bookshelf door.

"Don't mind him. We all made this decision equally. We all fucked up, and now you're our responsibility to keep safe," Colson said, breaking the silence in the room. Everett continued to hold my face, easing my anxiety about all that had occurred tonight.

"He's right, you'll be safe with us, even though we're the ones who caused all this."

"What do you guys mean?" Tears started to escape my eyes as exhaustion slowly took hold of my body. I was beyond tired. I was running on pure adrenaline at that point, and my body was slowly coming down from the high I was riding.

"We can talk about this after you get some rest. You're exhausted. Here, let me take you to your room."

I wanted to protest, but my body slowly betrayed me as I began shutting down. My muscles started to feel like jelly while the tension started easing its way from each muscle fiber. It took all my strength to try and keep my eyelids open. My eyes were still leaking with tears. I felt Everett's hands on my face again.

"Look at me, Sloan; you're safe with us. No one in this world will hurt you as long as you're with us. Call us your guardians. Now let's go. You're practically sleeping standing up." Everett scooped me into his arms and proceeded to carry me up the stairs with Colson trailing behind us. Everett's warm chest and the sound of his heart beating had me dozing off to sleep before we even made it to my room. I woke slightly when I felt the warmth of bed covers that were being pulled over me. A soft kiss heated my forehead.

"Goodnight, love," Everett whispered in my ear, and then he left me to sleep.

CHAPTER 12

SLOAN

My dreams were full of blood, lots of blood, pooling around my feet as I stared down at the ever-growing circle beneath me. My feet were bare and slowly disappearing beneath the warm, thick, dark blood. I looked up and saw bodies everywhere, scattered throughout the room I stood in. Panicking, I looked around and spotted three shadowy figures in the corner of the room—each holding pistols in their hands. I saw one of them lift their gun, pointing it right at me. My breathing grew rapidly, and suddenly, a loud shot rang through the air.

I jolted awake, sitting straight up in my bed, sweating and trying to catch my breath. I grabbed my face with my hands and closed my eyes as I started rubbing my temples.

"You okay?" I heard someone ask in a tired, sleep-filled voice beside me. Startled, I jumped again and turned to my side to see Everett lying right next to me. He was on his back with no shirt, and the sheet was just covering his junk.

Was he naked underneath? Damn, that's hot. Wait, what the fuck was he doing in here? His arms were folded behind his head, and his eyes were still closed, but he wasn't sleeping, since he was talking to me.

"What the fuck are you doing in my bed?" I yelled as I shoved the covers off myself and jumped out of bed. Looking down at myself, I saw that I was still wearing one of his white T-shirts and no pants, just my black cheeky panties that overly exposed a little too much of my ass. I guess that's why they call them cheeky panties. He turned on his side, facing me and propped his head on his hand. Looking me up and down as he let out a sleepy yawn.

"Just making sure you're safe, or did you forget about the people who came to kill you last night?"

"How do you know they weren't here to kill you guys?" I crossed my arms across my chest.

"Because we can't be killed, love."

I stared at him for a long while, curious as to what made these men so untouchable. Why were they trying to protect me? Who was I to them? These men were dangerous and knew how to kill people, but that still didn't explain why they thought they were responsible for protecting me? I needed answers, like now.

"Why are you guys protecting me? You don't even know me." My eyes wandered down his chiseled chest again, making me squeeze my thighs together. Every inch of his chest was covered in elaborate tattoos, dancing down his torso and dipping below the sheets. I wondered how far they went? *Stop it, Sloan, focus.* Blinking my eyes a few times, I looked back up at his face, and his smirk said it all. He knew I was checking him out. Busted. His piercing blue eyes were locked on me, and I couldn't help but bite my bottom lip.

A low groan came from his throat, and I looked back up at his face.

"Do that again, and I will bite it for you." His gaze was hard, and I felt my cheeks redden. He sat up in bed, still allowing the sheet to cover his package, and leaned against the headboard. He brushed his hair back from his head and patted the space beside him.

"Sit down, Sloan, and let me explain."

I hesitated for a second, but my curiosity wanted answers. I did as I was told and pulled back the covers to sit cross-legged beside him. I covered myself to try and hide that I was only wearing panties under my shirt, but I think he already knew by the way he was smirking at me—kind of hard not to notice since my legs were fully exposed. I leaned back on the headboard, as well, and crossed my arms across my chest and waited for him to speak.

He took a long sigh before speaking again. "Dean, Colson, and I were tasked with a job that we shouldn't have accepted. We are a part of an organization that takes down the world's most dangerous and notorious criminals who were deemed too dangerous for society. We were sent our targets, and it was our job to eliminate them. We were trained at a very young age. This was the life we were meant to live. Do we like to kill people? Not necessarily. But we do know the people we kill are bad, Sloan. The world is safer without them. We were sent an unusual job that was out of our usual job description."

"What was the job?" My voice trembled from the knowledge that these men were trained killers. That's what they did. They killed people, no questions asked.

"You were the job." His voice was steady and unflinching, and his gaze was focused straight ahead, not even turning to look at me.

"What the hell are you talking about? I'm the job?" My hands began sweating, and my chest heaved with anger.

"Yes, we were sent a job, a snatch and deliver. Something we don't do, but this was sent from the top, and in our organization, you don't ask questions. We were sent a photo and where you would be." Everett's hand brushed his hair back again. I was beginning to think this was a nervous habit. "We waited for you to get off work and followed you as you walked home. When you reached the alley, we grabbed you."

"Wait a minute. You didn't grab me. You fucking hit me over the head with something and knocked me the fuck out," I hissed at him, causing him to finally look at me. "Who was the asshole that hit me, and what did he hit me with?"

"That would be Dean. You started fighting back, and before you could make a scene, he hit the back of your head with his fist. He wasn't supposed to hit you, but you see, Dean is not the patient type."

"Yeah, no shit," I said under my breath.

"Once we delivered you to the drop point, we realized where they were taking you. We had no idea they wanted you for Stone Fortress. Once we handed you over, we knew we had to get you back before the auctions started." His voice was low, but I could hear the anger coming from his core.

"Why did you take me in the first place?"

"Sometimes high priority people go missing, such as politician's children who run away, and we are tasked with retrieving them. We thought you were some teenager who had just run off, and a rich family paid good money to have you returned. When it clicked that we had just kidnapped someone for Stone Fortress ... " Everett hesitated, and his arm muscles began to flex. I could feel the heat radiating from his body. His neck vein throbbed furiously, so I grabbed his hand and started rubbing the top of his palm, trying to ease his anger. It seemed to be working, and his arms slowly released their tension. Turning to look at me again, he continued,

"We are not the ones to be messed with, Sloan. They knew we wouldn't have taken you if we knew where you would end up. We knew we were going to get you back." He cupped my face with his large hand, but I jerked away from his touch.

They were the ones who kidnapped me. They stole me from the life I had worked so hard to create. If it weren't for them, I would be at work right now, making an honest living as a hardworking, independent woman. They stole that away from me. Anger flooded my core, and I jerked the covers off me, throwing my legs off the bed. Before I could stand up, his hand grabbed my wrist, holding me back. I tried yanking my hand from his, but his hold was too tight.

"Let me go, right fucking now, Everett!"

He didn't; he just kept his grip on me. I tried to pull away again, but I was met with an equally hard pull that had me fall back into his arms. His strong arms wrapped firmly around my chest, and I could feel the warmth of his breath on my ear. A shiver traveled throughout my body at his touch.

"You have every reason to be mad, but know if it weren't for us coming back for you, you would be some old man's sex slave right now. I wasn't going to let that happen to you." His lips brushed against my ear and down my neck.

My head tilted to the side, giving him better access to my neck, and I internally kicked myself for allowing my body to betray me.

"I will never ask you to do anything you don't want to. I am not like those men. I will wait until you ask for me—when you want me as much as I want you. Just tell me when, love."

He released me, and internally my body screamed in protest for him to come back, but he was already out of bed. He was in fact naked under the sheet, entirely and gorgeously naked. I turned and watched him walk away from the bed, toward the lounge chair placed in the room's corner. His back muscles flexed with every step he took. Even his ass had muscles. Shit, this man was a real-life Greek god. He picked up his jeans and threaded his legs through each opening. As he started buttoning up his pants, he turned toward me.

"I'll have new clothes for you soon. What are your sizes?"

I gave him a hard look before answering.

"Size 4 pants and size small tops." My voice was low.

"Help yourself to anything you want. You have your bathroom, and there will always be one of us here if you need anything. You will be staying with us until we can ensure you will be safe and the threat is eliminated." He was still shirtless—thank God for that—as he made his way back over to me. He knelt in front of the bed where I was sitting and rested his arms on his knees. Looking at me with his liquid-blue eyes, he said, "You're safer here with us for the time being. I know you don't want that, but I can't risk your safety because of my mistake." He stood up and threaded his fingers through the back of my head, pulling me toward him. He kissed my forehead so tenderly that I welcomed his embrace.

Releasing me, he made his way toward the bedroom door.

"Take your time in here. I'm going to make breakfast when you're ready." He left the room, leaving me pissed and highly turned on. What the fuck was wrong with me? Sitting back on the bed, I allowed myself to absorb all he had admitted to me. They were the ones who had kidnapped me and brought me to that dungeon of a castle. They were also the ones to come back and save me from a fate worse than death. He was right. I am allowed to be mad; they stole my life from me and now there are others coming for me. Then again, if they weren't the ones to kidnap me, then someone else would have. And who's to say they would have felt remorse and come back to retrieve me?

I do feel safe here; they all showed their loyalty last night by protecting me from whomever the hell was trying to come for me. They want to protect me. They want me here. And to be honest with myself, I want to be here as well. They make me feel…untouchable.

CHAPTER 13

SLOAN

I took my time in the bath, allowing the water to ease the tension in my shoulders. The enormous tub swallowed me whole as lavender-scented bubbles concealed my body. Leaning my head back, I closed my eyes and thought of what Everett admitted to me earlier. Everett, Colson, and Dean were the ones who had kidnapped me—snatched me off the streets and robbed me of an average life. I wanted to be angry, but I was aware that they had come back for me. They were given minimal information about the job, and once they realized where I was going to end up, they came back for me. Then again, if it weren't for them, I wouldn't be in this situation in the first place. My head started hurting as I tried to unscramble the mess that was my brain.

Just then, a knock at the door and the twisting of

the knob had me jolt in the tub, causing water to splash on the floor.

"Knock, knock, sweetheart, we come bearing gifts." Colson walked into the room, followed by Dean. Both guys were carrying what looked to be shopping bags—and a lot of them.

"Umm, kind of busy here and kind of naked." I looked through to the bedroom, as both of them stopped dead in their tracks and stared at me soaking in the tub. Colson just smiled his devilishly handsome smile, while Dean expressed no emotion with his handsomely stoic face. Does this man ever smile?

"Hey, gorgeous, need some company? I could help wash your hair." Colson dropped the bags in his hands and started walking toward the bathroom's entrance. I looked over his shoulder and saw Dean put his bags down as well and begin following Colson.

"I'm a big girl, boys. I think I can manage a bath on my own, thanks." However, a bath with two sexy as hell men would put me in a good mood. I shook my head, trying to stop the visual of them naked that was forming in my head.

"Are you sure? You don't sound too convincing." Colson was now standing right beside the tub, looking down at me. I have never been more thankful for bubbles in my life as I was in that moment. I had filled the bath with so many bubbles that my body was completely hidden beneath the suds. I gave him an amused smirk as I turned and saw Dean leaning against the doorframe to the bathroom.

"Everett told us he explained everything to you," Dean finally spoke as he crossed his arms in front of his chest. I nodded my head, not sure what to say. Colson then sat on the floor and leaned his back against the porcelain of the tub. I looked between the both of them as sorrow filled their faces.

"I'm so sorry we've done this to you. It wasn't supposed to happen this way." Colson's voice, full of regret. I looked at the side of his face as he looked down at the floor, not wanting to meet my eyes. I drifted my gaze to Dean, and he was also looking at the floor.

"Listen, what you guys did was truly fucked up, and it's put me in this situation where I don't know what to do next. Everett also told me you all came back for me instead of letting me become some play toy for whoever had the highest bid. I can't dwell on the past because nothing can be changed now. I have to look to the future, and right now, I'm just glad I'm not in the hands of some greedy piece of shit, doing whatever he wants to me. I'm still mad at you guys, really fucking mad, but I guess I can kick the shit out of you all later." I looked between them both, their gaze now resting on me.

I heard the sound of footsteps and saw Everett walking up behind Dean. "Is there a party in here or what?" Everett asked, his hands in his jean pockets and a half smile gracing his perfect face.

"Oh, you know, they're just begging for my forgiveness after ruining my life. Care to join?" I smiled jokingly at him. He let out a small chuckle as all three men were now staring at me. Looking down at my body, I noticed the bubbles had started to dissipate. "Unless you all want a show, I suggest you leave me be so I can finish up."

"I like shows," Colson spoke up, smiling big until Dean whacked the side of his head with his hand.

"Come on, you idiot. Let her get dressed in peace." Dean turned and made his way out of the room. Colson followed him, but not before turning his head and giving me a wink. Everett was still in the doorway, his eyes roaming the bubble-infested water. His gaze caused the dormant butterflies in my stomach to go insane. I squeezed my legs together as his eyes reached my face.

"You've got you some new clothes, shoes, panties, and bras. We weren't sure of what you like, so we got a little bit of everything. If you need anything else, just let me know, and I'll get it for you. Breakfast is ready downstairs whenever you're hungry." Everett gave the water one last glance before turning in the doorway to leave.

"Everett?" I called after him. He turned and met my gaze.

"Why are you doing all this for me?"

"Because, like I, said this is our mistake, and I will do anything and everything to make sure you're safe. You don't deserve this life." He brushed his hair back.

"We will make sure you are taken care of and kept safe from here on out; you don't have to worry anymore." He turned and left, and I let out the breath I didn't realize I'd been holding.

Getting out of the bathtub, I wrapped my body in a towel as I stared at my reflection in the mirror. A few days ago, I was Sloan, the barista who had escaped her abusive family to start her own life in Europe. Now, I was Sloan, the kidnapped American girl who'd barely escaped a sex trafficking ring and was now being guarded by three insanely handsome men, waiting on me hand and foot. If that wasn't the most fucked-up story you'd heard, I don't know what was. Coming from nothing and no one to now having three guardians of my own … I guess I could get used to this.

CHAPTER 14

DEAN

She seemed so unafraid, so unaffected. What had happened to this girl to make her not fear death? I wanted nothing to do with her the second we took her, but her willingness to accept our apology so quickly had me thinking differently of her. If I were in her shoes, I couldn't say I would be accepting of the situation. I admired her strength and willingness to move forward instead of focusing on the path that had brought her here.

Watching her in the tub, I had taken in her beauty. Her hair was in a messy bun on top of her head, with loose strands framing her face. Her collarbone and the top of her shoulders were the only bit of skin I could see above the colossal number of bubbles she'd created. I had hoped the bubbles would've quickly disappeared. My eyes burned to see the rest of her. Now and then, she'd raised one foot just enough to see her toes appear from beneath the suds. She was breathtaking.

As I watched her turn her head when she spoke, I noticed the faint detail of a scar on one of her shoulders. Staring, I noticed the shape looked oddly familiar to something I'd seen before. It was round, roughly the size of a dime or penny. The center was more profound than the rest, and the skin within it looked like burn marks. Just as she lifted her neck a little higher out of the water, it dawned on me. That was a cigar burn. Someone had put a burning cigar to her skin to cause pain, to torture her. I rubbed my finger along the same scar located on my right forearm. I'd received my mark when I was about ten years old. In one of his drunken stupors, my old man decided to see how long it would take for me to cry while he held his cigar to my arm. As it burned through the layers of my skin, my screams did nothing to stop him. One of many scars that piece of shit gave me before I escaped his torment.

Looking at Sloan now, I felt the pain of my scar burn as I tried to imagine who would do this to her. Whoever it was, I wanted to find them and return the favor. I wanted to destroy the person who had ever lain hands on her. She would never know that type of pain again, not while I was here. As much as I felt like this was a mistake, her being here, I had to admit, this was our wrongdoing. She was just the poor girl stuck in the crossfire. It was our job now to protect her, to keep her safe. We had fucked up, but we'd also be the ones to make things right. She was safe with us.

———

COLSON

Sitting on the tile floor next to Sloan, I listened as she accepted the half-assed apology we gave her. Well, the apology I gave her. Dean was just standing in the doorway looking like the big ass brute he is. I hated to admit it, but I was almost happy this whole situation had happened because now she was here with us. Call me selfish, but I wanted to keep her. She had this gravitational pull on me, and the further I got from her, the stronger the force became. I wanted to touch her, hold her, taste her on my lips. I wanted to worship her tight little body and protect her from all things that could go bump in the night. She was my girl now, our girl, and no one was taking her away from us now. She may have gotten here by our stupidity, but I didn't regret a thing. If it weren't for that stupid ass job, she would still be brewing coffee at that little shop on the corner, and I wouldn't be on the floor beside her, watching her bathe. Yeah, I'm selfish, but I know what I want, and that's her.

———

EVERETT

She was so relaxed, as three men, who were strangers to her a few days ago, stood around and watched her soak in bubbles. The tension from the morning's nightmare had seemed to ease from her shoulders, as steam from the water rose. Her face was calm, and her blue eyes stared right into my soul. I hated that we did this to her, but I didn't regret bringing her here. She was safe with us—guarded and protected from evil. An evil that would have taken hold of her if she'd stayed at Stone Fortress.

Staring at her lips, I couldn't help but remember the feeling of them pressed against mine. Her taste left me wanting more, and seeing her in the tub now —so vulnerable, so exposed—was making my cock hard beneath my tight jeans. Leaving her to finish up, I turned and headed back down to the kitchen to join the guys. I saw how they both looked at her; they wanted her just as much as I did. We'd fallen for the job—something we'd vowed never to do. She was the job, but now she was ours. No one would ever fuck with her again, not if I had anything to do about it.

CHAPTER 15

SLOAN

I look through the endless bags of clothes the guys brought to my room; they spared no expense. When I finally can't decide on what to wear, I settle for a pair of black jeans and a gray long-sleeved shirt. I don't bother doing my hair; I just simply run a comb through it and let it air dry. My stomach starts growling, so I hang up my towel and head down the hallway to the stairs. Walking barefoot down the hallway, I dig my toes into the plush carpet that extends throughout the second floor. Reaching the stairs, I hear the faint mumble of the guys conversing in the kitchen, so I make my way down the grand staircase and through the arched doorway of the kitchen.

As soon as I walk in, all conversation stops, and their eyes are on me.

"Well, no need to stop talking just because I showed up. Unless you were talking about me."

Sauntering over to the island, I pull out a barstool and take a seat.

Dean is sitting on the countertop, sipping from his coffee mug, and Colson is standing at the end of the island, shoveling waffles into his mouth so fast I wonder if he is even breathing. He's also shirtless, and I try not to be too obvious when I stare at his chiseled abs that flex with every movement he makes. Everett stands up from the barstool he was sitting on. He fills a plate with waffles and strawberries and then drizzles syrup over the top. He slides me the plate.

"Eat, love. You must be starving." He smiles at me as he turns and starts filling another mug with coffee. I smile back as I pick up my fork, cut into the perfect fluffy waffles, and take a large mouthful. I let out a moan of satisfaction and dive in for another bite.

"Jesus, that sound was hot." I look up and see Colson leaning over the island, staring at me. I shoot him a wink before I continue inhaling my waffles. Everett sets a cup of coffee in front of me as he takes his seat next to me.

It doesn't take me long to finish my waffles. I was truly starving. Pushing the plate away, I lean back in my chair and start sipping my coffee. I look up from my cup and meet all three of the guys' gazes still on me.

"Umm, so I know we all met under the most insane circumstances, but I wanted to say thank you for coming back for me. Although you did kidnap me first, you also didn't have to come back for me. I thank you for that, and thank you for protecting me last night from whoever the fuck those guys were." I look from one to the other but stop on Everett. His blue eyes are like crystals that cut into my core.

Just as the silence was getting to be too much, Colson stands up from the island. "Well, we honestly don't deserve a thank you, but you're welcome, sweetheart!" Walking over to me, he picks me up from my stool and swings me around. His body is warm—hot even, like he has his own internal furnace and it's turned up to the max temperature.

"Put her down, you idiot. You're squeezing her too hard. She can't breathe," Dean says over his coffee mug.

"Oh shit. My bad." He puts me back on my feet, and I turn to Dean and give him a silent thank you.

Just then, Everett's phone rings. Before answering the call, he turns to Dean.

"Dean, show her around the house. Colson and I have to talk with Max about the new security upgrades around the property. Let's go, Colson." Everett then accepts the call on his phone. I look to Colson, who looks bummed he isn't the one to show me around the house. Giving me another one of his sexy winks, he turns and follows Everett out of the kitchen. Once they've left the kitchen, I turn and see Dean has already hopped off the counter and is making his way over to my side.

"All right then, you're mine for the morning."

Crossing the room toward me, he stops inches

away from me, looking down at me as I crane my neck to look up at him. He lifts his mug and takes a long sip as his scent takes hold of my nose. He smells of fresh soap and pine. Inhaling all that's Dean, I close my eyes for a second and try steadying my brain that is wandering off to all my naughty fantasies.

"Let's go then," he says to me, breaking me from my distracting thoughts.

Dean takes me throughout the main level of the house, showing me another living room that doesn't look like it gets much use; instead it's all for show. I guess you would call it their formal living room. Then takes me through the garage that connects to their gym. The gym is enormous, filled with all the free weights, cable machines, and cardio equipment you can imagine—the whole room is lined with mirrors, making it seem even more significant than it already is.

After he shows me around the gym, he takes me through a door that leads to the backyard. As we step outside, my mouth drops as I see their Olympic-size pool.

"Holy shit," I softly let out, not expecting Dean to hear me.

"What?" he replies, looking back at me from where he stands.

"This pool is massive. Why do you need an Olympic-size pool in your backyard?" I meet his gaze as he turns his body toward me.

"Why not?

"Touché. Is it heated?" I ask, hoping he will say yes. I lean down to touch the water before he even has time to answer. It's warm, just as warm as the bath I took earlier this morning. "Can I go for a swim sometime?" I look over my shoulder at him as he's standing with his hands in his pockets, studying me.

"Are you some sort of swimmer?" He asks, tilting his head slightly.

"I swam in high school. It was the only sport that went on all year long. It allowed me to stay longer at school every day instead of going straight home." I look back at the crystal water as I answer his question, not wanting him to see my face. Swimming allowed me extra time away from my chaotic home life. I would do anything to stay away from my parents as long as I could.

"Why didn't you want to go home, Sloan?" His voice, low and demanding.

I don't answer him right away. I just brush my fingers along the surface of the water, causing ripples to form. I hear him walking closer behind me, and then he kneels beside me.

"Sloan, tell me why you didn't want to go home?" His eyes are locked on me, patiently awaiting my response.

"My parents are bad people; that's all, Dean." I don't want to go into detail just to relive the horrors of my childhood. I take my hand out of the water and dry it on my jeans.

"Are they the ones who gave you that cigar burn on your shoulder?"

I freeze, not realizing he'd noticed my imperfection. I turn my face toward him, and he's rolling up his sleeve on his left arm.

"We all have a past, Sloan, full of secrets and memories we wish we could forget." His sleeve reaches just above his elbow, displaying an identical burn on his forearm. "Don't let them take away from you more than they already have." I gape at his burn. He has a past, as do I. A dark past where monsters live in the human form. A past where pain and torture are abundant each and every day. "Our past makes us stronger, Sloan. We are stronger than most people because we survived. You are a survivor, remember that." He rolls his sleeve down and gets to his feet. "Come, let me show you the rest of the house." I follow Dean back inside.

CHAPTER 16

SLOAN

Dean continues to show me the rest of the house. The upstairs consists of all our bedrooms and a few spare bedrooms as well. There's a movie room with a massive sectional and a television that stretches the length of the wall. The corner of the movie room is a makeshift concession stand with a popcorn machine and an assortment of candies displayed neatly behind a glass cupboard.

We don't talk much for the rest of the tour. I want to know more about Dean, who he is and where he came from. What makes this man so sweet, yet so bitter at times. He seems to care for me, but he is also annoyed I am here. He makes me nervous being around him at times, but I also feel incredibly safe in his presence. Before I know it, we are back in the kitchen, and the other two are still not back from wherever they went.

"You have free rein of the house, Sloan. Help yourself to whatever you like." He opens the fridge and grabs two water bottles for us.

"What are you going to do now?" I ask him, opening my bottle and taking a sip of the ice-cold water.

"Well, the guys will be working out the security for the rest of the morning. I'll probably just play some video games until they're done, and they'll fill me in on everything they learned." He walks over to the game console and powers it on. "Want to play?" he asks me over his shoulder.

I consider his offer for a moment but then ask, "Do you mind if I take a swim? Swimming helps clear my head." I fiddle with my water bottle before I hear him chuckle under his breath. He sets the remote down and walks right up to me.

"You don't need to ask permission, doll. You aren't our prisoner. Knock yourself out." He tucks a loose strand of my hair behind my ear and brushes his thumb down my cheek.

I welcome his touch and lean into his thumb before he drops his hand. The slightest touch from these men has me melting in their palms like butter. Can you blame me, though? All three of them look like they should be gracing the cover of a *GQ* magazine, apart from all their tattoos covering 90 percent of their bodies. I bite my bottom lip, nervous at how close we are standing. I can feel his heat coming off his body. His gray eyes have me mesmerized as I continue to stare at his gorgeous face.

"Why are you so nervous around me, Sloan?" he asks in a low, seductive tone.

I take in a few breaths before responding. "I-I don't know," I answer honestly, closing my eyes as I try to pull myself together. He cups my chin in his hand and tilts my head toward his.

"Look at me," he demands. Opening my eyes, I see his face is mere centimeters from mine, our lips practically touching. "You don't have to be afraid of us, Sloan. We will never do anything to hurt you again." He closes the gap between us, our lips crashing together as he threads his fingers through my hair and holds me still. He parts our lips, and his tongue massages against mine. He grabs my face with both of his hands and pulls me in deeper; our bodies flush against one another. His touch ignites a fire in my core and has my pussy throbbing. I want more. Just then, he releases me, pulling my face away from his to stare down at me. We are both panting as he rests his forehead on mine.

"Be careful swimming. There is no lifeguard on duty. Unless you need me to save you." With that, he gives me a sheepish smile and turns to head back to the couch. I'm left standing there with a severe case of blue vulva.

What is wrong with me, I think to myself as I make my way upstairs to my designated room. First Everett, now Dean. I've kissed two men that occupy this house, so what does that make me? I can't help my attraction to these three. They've saved my life twice so far. I mean the first time was warranted, since they were the ones to kidnap me in the first place. The second, well they didn't have to protect me from… whoever tried to kill me. Will Everett be mad that Dean and I kissed? We aren't together, so he shouldn't be, right? I'm not with any of them; I'm simply just staying in their house until "the threat" is handled. *Damn it, Sloan.*

I pulled out a bathing suit from one of the bags the guys had brought to my room. Looking it over, I smiled to myself as I turned over the barely there fabric between my fingers. It's a red two-piece with cheeky bottoms and tiny triangle pieces that look like they would hardly cover my nipples. Leave it to three men to choose a bathing suit for a woman.

I guess if they are stuck with me, they mind as well get a show every now and then. Smart men. After I got it on, I threw on the robe that was hanging in my bathroom and made my way back downstairs. I walked down the hallway that led to the gym and exited the side door. I set my towel down on the side of the pool and let my legs dangle in the water. It was around lunchtime, but the air was still a brisk and chilly autumn day even though the sun was out. The water, on the other hand, was warm—almost too warm. I pulled the hair tie out of my hair, which had been holding my hair in a messy bun, and placed the hair tie on my wrist instead.

Taking a few deep breaths, I hopped over the edge of the pool and submerged myself, welcoming the heat of the water as it danced over my body. I kept myself submerged, allowing the silence to fill my ears and soothe my body. The eerie silence the water held beneath its surface was one of the many things I enjoyed about swimming. It felt as if I were in an alternate universe. The world's usual sounds around me were cut off and gave me a sense of serenity that nothing else could.

Breaking the surface and inhaling a deep breath of the bitter air, I opened my eyes, looking out into the forest behind the house. I was greeted by the sound of leaves rustling from the wind and a few birds singing their familiar songs. The leaves were already changing colors from vibrant green to warm tones of orange and yellow. Wading in the water, I tilt my head back once more, allowing the water to pull, ever so lightly, on my hair as it sinks beneath its surface.

How did I get here? I'd never been the one to feel sorry for myself, but at this moment, I welcomed the feeling of pity. I'd never been the person on the right side of luck or the person who'd been dealt a winning hand. I had always struggled, fought, and survived day by day. Growing up under my parent's abusive touch was the foundation of the person that was me. Their brutality and neglect created a wall of a structure that blocked any and everything that could and would hurt me. I trusted no one. Even now, with three strange men, I had accepted their apology, but did I trust them? They protected me on the first night's invasion, but was that a mask to break my wall down and allow them in? What about the kiss Dean just delivered to me? Was that his way of distracting me from whatever their plan was?

I held my breath and submerged my mouth and nose in the pool stopping just below my eyes. I watched the leaves move in the wind as I waded in the water. I allowed the familiar burn of my muscles to begin to ache and fill my fibers. My mind was a whirlwind of confusion and self-doubt. I shouldn't trust these men. I'd grown up never trusting anyone, so why should these men be any different? Making up my mind, I started freestyle swimming up and down the center of the pool. My mind soon went numb, and I focused solely on my strokes and breath as my rhythm took its course.

After roughly two hours, I found myself indeed spent and exhausted from my swim. My arms and legs were tense, as the lactic acid set in, causing my muscles to burn from the constant resistance of the water. My abs were exposed to their full potential as I lifted my body from the water and walked the perimeter of the pool, fetching my towel.

Drying off my face and wrapping the towel around my now cold body, I looked down to the concrete and froze. Beneath me, a giant rusty-brown stain was visible on the concrete. Remembering this was the spot where one of the intruders had been shot, I felt my stomach start to turn, as bile made its way up my stomach and traveled to my esophagus.

Remaining frozen to that spot, I remembered what his body had looked like on the security monitor and how the blood had pooled so quickly around his life-less body. I couldn't hold back any longer, the bile reached the top of my esophagus, and I turned to find the closest bush. Making it to the edge of the forest behind the house, I hunched over, emptying the contents of my stomach. I stayed like that until I heard Everett's voice.

"Must have been one serious swim for you to be throwing up so hard." Everett's words rang out over the short distance from the pool to where I was stand-ing. I wiped my mouth on the edge of my towel and made my way over to him. He was leaning against the small building I guessed was the pool house. His arms crossed over his broad frame, exposing his well-defined biceps. He was wearing a pair of dark jeans and a white V-neck shirt. A grin stretched across his face as if he was trying to hold back his laughter.

"Yeah, I guess I just pushed myself a little too hard." Not wanting to admit the actual reason why I'd gotten sick, I grabbed my robe and threaded my arms through it, tying a knot in the front. "How were the security updates?" I asked, not knowing what else to say. I pulled my hair back into its usual messy bun style and secured it with my hair tie.

"Quite well. We were able to improve the silent alarm by stretching the parameter further, as well as more security cameras and motion sensor devices throughout the property. I've also assembled a more reliable security group that will be on a rotation, so we are guarded at all times."

"I thought I was safe with the three of you," I asked sarcastically, turning to face him. He gave me a half smile,

"You are, love. I thought we displayed that well last night." His gaze was locked on me as he stepped closer. I returned the look, not wanting to seem intimidated by his presence.

"You're not afraid of us, are you?"

False. I am afraid. I am afraid of these three murderous, kidnapping, gorgeous strangers who now want to protect me. I'm afraid that I'm lying to myself and I'm not actually as afraid as I should be. But I wouldn't admit this to any of them.

"No, why? Should I be?" I gave him a slight head tilt and pinched my eyebrows together, looking up at him with a confused expression.

"As much as I want to believe you, your body language tells me otherwise."

I was standing with my arms crossed, and one of my legs was crossed over the other. How could the way I was standing make me look scared?

"You must be reading me wrong." I rolled my eyes, trying harder to appear unamused.

"Your breathing is unbalanced, and you're squeezing your arms more and more the closer I step toward you. Maybe it's the way you bite your bottom lip before you respond. It's OK if you are scared. Most people are afraid."

Shit, he was good. I hadn't realized how my body was responding until now. My fingers were aching at how hard I was squeezing my biceps. I needed to work on my body language in front of them.

"I think you want me scared. I think you want me to be like everyone else and cower just from the sight of you."

He let out a small laugh. "Quite the opposite. I want you to trust me. To trust that we brought you here to protect you. I want you to be comfortable around us and let us care for you to make up for the trauma we caused you for those few days in Stone Fortress. Let us make up for our mistakes." He spoke softly in a soothing tone that had me fidgeting where I stood.

"To trust someone is to make myself vulnerable. To survive this world, I never expect protection from anyone else but myself."

"Then why do you stay?" He narrowed his eyes.

"I ... um ... will you let me leave? I was under the impression I was to stay here until you deemed it safe for me to go?"

"If you are confident you can protect yourself from the evils that are sure to hunt you, be my guest. The door is open." He was serious. He stepped back a step and uncrossed his arms.

I was free to go. Was this a test? Could I protect myself? The invitation was open, and I didn't want him thinking I was a liar and couldn't handle myself. With that, I turned and started walking back to the house to get my things and leave. Before I even made it to the door, he spoke again.

"Know this, Sloan. Last night was just a taste of what kind of people are hunting you. You think Stone Fortress was a nightmare before? If those men catch you, they will show you no mercy. Torture is their specialty, and to send a message to you and us, they will make sure your death is excruciatingly painful."

His warning left me immobile. I was no stranger to pain, but his words had me second-guessing myself. I felt him before I heard him. His body was now behind me as he fiddled with a loose strand of my hair.

"I know you are strong, love. I saw it in your eyes when you ran out of the Fortress. With your determination, your strength, and the fight vibrating off your body, I admired your will to live. I know you're not a weak woman, Sloan. Just let us help you and keep you safe for now. There will be time for running and creating yourself again, but for now, let us be your saviors."

I closed my eyes as I let his words sink in. His arm snaked around my waist, and he turned me to face him. His crystal eyes were hard on me, a silent plea to stay with them.

"Okay, fine. I will stay. Just know this is not permanent. I am gone the moment it's safe to leave."

My words were harsh, but he just smiled down at me as if he'd won.

"We will see about that." He cupped my face with his hand, wiping a droplet of water that had made its way to my cheek. Bringing my face to his, he kissed the top of my forehead before resting his head against mine.

"Let's get something to eat. I'm starving." With that he stepped away from me heading toward the door. Opening it and waiting for me to enter first, he gave me a cheeky smile. I guess chivalry isn't dead after all.

CHAPTER 17

SLOAN

With Colson and Dean, we decided that we would go out to eat at one of their favorite places, a small Italian restaurant on the outskirts of town. Dean was very much against leaving the house. He insisted that it was too dangerous and that we needed to continue to lie low. Thankfully, with a lot of begging from Colson, the decision was made. I headed upstairs to change, with a little more bounce to my step. Excited to be leaving the house and venture around town had me smiling from ear to ear. Apart from Dean's fear of it being too dangerous, I was genuinely excited to feel like a normal human being again. Enough of this feeling of being a prisoner or being someone else's property. I was ready to feel the wind on my face, smell the scents of the town, and have no walls to box me in, holding me hostage.

I decided to wear something simple, a plain gray

dress with spaghetti straps that dipped low in the back. These men did indeed have great taste in clothes. I gave myself a mental reminder to properly thank them for my new wardrobe. I paired my dress with a pair of black booties with a slight heel and styled my hair in loose beach waves. Looking in the mirror, I saw Sloan. I felt like myself again—a young woman ready for a night out on the town. The feeling of ecstasy flowed through my veins as I gave myself a last look and headed for the door.

Making my way down the hall, I could hear the guys already downstairs, talking among themselves. I headed down the stairs and turned toward the kitchen. I'd come to realize this was their usual gathering room. While I crossed the threshold to the kitchen, all eyes turned to me.

They were holding open beers. I scanned each of them, noticing how truly handsome and godlike they were. Colson had his hair in a man bun, loose with strands escaping his hair tie. He was wearing dark jeans and a tight V-neck white T-shirt, which displayed all of his juicy abdominal muscles.

Dean was also in dark jeans, paired with a long-sleeved black shirt. A chain reached from his back pocket to his front pocket. Then there was Everett, the picture of elegance, wearing black slacks and a long-sleeved button-down shirt. The sleeves were rolled up, and I could see all his forearm tattoos on display.

"Damn, gorgeous, look at you," Colson gawked as he placed his beer on the island and made his way over to me. He then grabbed my hand and spun me around, whistling as he took in the back of my dress. Smiling, I let him twirl me while I took in the sight of these three men who had changed my life in such a short amount of time.

"This isn't a good idea, Everett," Dean said under his breath. He rubbed his shaved head with his hand before tipping back the rest of his beer, emptying the contents.

"Give her this one night of normalcy. She deserves that much. We'll all be guarding her; she's not alone." I heard Everett reply to Dean. At that statement, I smiled harder, knowing they were with me, protecting me and ensuring my safety, which only awakened the butterflies in my core. Colson stopped spinning me. He then leaned in, hugging me and lifting me off the ground.

"You look stunning, love." He planted a kiss on my cheek before letting me down.

"All right then, are we ready to go?" I made eye contact with each of them.

With that, Colson took my hand again and led the way to the garage. The other two grabbed their jackets and followed us. With his free hand, Colson clicked a button on his key fob. The lights of a Mercedes G-Wagon illuminated the garage, and the engine roared as it started up. I gawked at the Mercedes and its slick black color, secretly wishing they would let me drive it or one of their many vehicles.

Colson opened the back door and helped me into the back seat. Kissing my hand before letting go, he met my eyes and gave me a seductive wink. He then got into the driver's seat. Everett climbed into the passenger seat, and Dean slid into the occupied seat beside me. He scooted in close to me—close enough that his thigh rested against mine. My breath hitched as his warmth engulfed my leg. I looked at him, but he was facing forward with an emotionless expression on his face. His jaw tensed as I saw the muscles flex every time he clenched his jaw. I reached over and place my hand on his thigh, drawing his attention to me.

"It will be okay." I said it low enough so that only he could hear. His smoldering gray eyes locked on me, not fully believing my reassurance. His face was still unreadable as he looked down at my hand, now rubbing gently against his jeans. His chest rose and fell with each breath. His massive frame looked cramped in the seat beside me. My lips started to tingle, remembering our kiss in the kitchen earlier today. Licking my lips, I looked away and focused on the trees passing outside.

We drove for about thirty minutes, listening to the radio as it filled the vehicle. We pulled into a small parking lot, and I turned my eyes and saw a small building made of large stones and draped in greenery. It was a beautiful quaint building. A sign was illuminated above it that read Rocco's. I adjusted my dress and then felt Colson's hand on my lower back as we started making our way toward the restaurant. Everett took the lead, and Dean fell in behind us. I couldn't help but feel a sense of security as Colson, Dean, and Everett caged me in with their massive frames.

Walking into the restaurant, I started examining my surroundings. I saw that the inside was just as charming as the outside. Smiling, I felt Colson's hand usher me forward to a table that was located toward the back of the building.

"We aren't going to wait for the hostess?" I asked, looking up at Colson. He didn't look down at me, just smiled as we continued to the table. It was a half-circle booth table, and Everett took the edge seat, waving me to scoot into the half circle chair. I slid in after him, then Colson. Dean sat on the edge, facing Everett. An older Italian gentleman noticed our entrance and made his way over to us, smiling wide. He slung a white hand towel over his shoulder and stretched out his arms.

"My boys, it's been too long." The gentlemen addressed the table as Everett reached over to shake his hand.

"Rocco, nice to see you. How's business been?" Everett asked Rocco, smiling just slightly.

"Wonderful, just wonderful, my boy. The usual, I presume?" He looked between the guys, smiling and making eye contact with each of them, stopping as he noticed me.

"My lady, I apologize I did not see you there,"

Rocco reached his hand across toward me, and I outstretched mine as well. Grabbing my hand, he kissed the top of my knuckles. "My name is Rocco. Please, whatever you need, let me know. If these three give you any trouble … " He shook his other hand in a fist-like motion, joking with the table. I smiled at him as he released my hand.

"This is Sloan," Everett introduced me to Rocco. Rocco's eyes lit up as he looked me over.

"That is a beautiful name for a beautiful lady. I will grab your drinks. Give me one moment." He then turned and made his way to the kitchen.

Colson and Dean were stretched out in the booth with their legs spread wide. Colson's arms were on the back of the chair, with one draped over my shoulder.

Rocco returned to the table almost immediately with four glasses of water. He placed the glasses one by one on the table.

"I already placed your order. It will be ready shortly."

"Thank you, Rocco," Everett said with a smile filling his face.

We sat in silence for a moment as I let my eyes wander the restaurant. The ambience was warm, and the lights were dim as they illuminated the place just enough. I started sipping my water when another waiter brought over a basket of buttered bread with a small bowl of seasoned oil. My stomach growled at the sight of the bread, and I wasted no time as I reached for a small saucer plate. I placed a piece on my plate and ripped a bit off. Dipping it into the oil, I dabbed the sides on the bowl, so no excess fell. Taking a small bite, I moaned in satisfaction. I was hungrier than I had thought.

"Jesus, Sloan. Those sounds are seriously hot," Colson said as he tilted his head back onto the backrest. I let out a small chuckle before apologizing.

"No need to apologize. Just know, it's doing things to my body every time you moan." Colson's lips were at my ear as he spoke in a low, hoarse voice. Closing my eyes, I felt goose flesh prickle my skin. I took a sip of my water, trying to calm the heat building in my core. I needed to collect myself and not let these men affect me with just their words. I had to remember I was not fully trusting of them—not just yet, that is.

The food arrived, breaking me out of my lust-filled trance, as Rocco placed plates of parmesan chicken, spaghetti and meatballs, lasagna, and three-cheese ravioli on the table. I took in the massive amount of food each plate held. I definitely wouldn't be finishing all the food that was piled high on my plate. We each thanked Rocco for his attentiveness.

"I hope you all enjoy, please let me know if you need anything else." He then excused himself from our table. Before eating, I, too, excused myself so I could use the restroom. Colson and Dean both stood from the booth, allowing me to slide out, but Dean began following me toward the restrooms.

"You don't need to escort me. I will be okay. I

promise." Looking to Dean, I saw him look over my shoulder to Everett, who shook his end. I guessed that meant I was okay to go alone because Dean then sat back down.

"Be quick," he said, nodding his head in the direction of the restroom.

I shot him a quick smile over my shoulder, reassuring him I would be fine. I found the restroom, located toward the opposite side of where we sat, tucked away in the corner. I pushed the door open to reveal a small two-stall restroom with a small vanity. Taking care of business, I made my way to the vanity to wash up. Watching the bubbles coat my hands, I continued to rub them together methodically before allowing the water to wash them away. I reached for the paper towels, when I noticed a shadow in the large mirror in front of me.

Looking into the mirror, I saw a man—actually two men. The twins from Stone Fortress! Stefan and Jei were right behind me, with evil smiles plastering their faces. I began opening my mouth to yell, but one of them—not sure which—clasped a hand over my mouth, wrapping his other hand around my arms.

"Did you think you wouldn't see us again, firecracker?" he whispered in my ear as the other pulled my arms behind me and secured them together with a zip tie. I tried fighting against his grasp, but he was too strong. He squeezed me tighter and pulled my head back against his chest, continuing to hold his hand over my mouth. My heart started racing as I tried screaming against his hand.

"No one will hear you, little one. We will be long gone before your boys even notice." His voice was evil, and I caught the hint of a chuckle escape his throat. He started dragging me from the restroom, and the other opened the door in front of us. Pulling me to the back door, I searched for the guys, but I was not in their line of sight. I should have let Dean come with me. What the fuck was I thinking? I cursed myself mentally, continuing to fight against the twins. He dragged me through the kitchen and out the back door, where a black SUV was idly waiting. Before he threw me in the vehicle, he secured a thick black strip of tape over my mouth, forbidding me from screaming.

This shit couldn't be happening to me. Not again. Kicking and thrashing back and forth, I tried to get myself free of his hold, but his strength overpowered me, and I was quickly thrown into the back seat. Slamming the door behind me, the other twin jumped in the driver seat and the other in the passenger seat. I heard the vehicle shift into drive. Tears started filling my eyes as the realization of being kidnapped again started to sink in.

Just as the vehicle began to pick up speed, I was thrown forward, rolling off the seat and hitting the SUV's floor. I hit my head on the center console, and I cursed the pain. Someone grabbed my legs and yanked me from the vehicle before I could even register what the fuck had just happened. I heard him before I saw him—Colson. His hands were grabbing my waist as he spun my body around to face him.

"Are you okay, sweetheart?" His tone was stern while he ripped the tape from my face.

"Ouch! What the fuck!" I screamed out. He cut the zip ties from my wrist before pulling me away from the vehicle. I turned to see that the SUV had driven straight into the side of another car that had pulled in front of the alleyway. After I inspected the SUV, I saw Dean. He was standing over the top of one of the twins, his fist viciously striking the twin's face, as blood splattered all over the both of them. I couldn't see Everett but imagined he was putting a beating on the other twin as well.

Colson had us sprinting around the building, when the sight of our Mercedes came into view. Approaching the vehicle, Colson ripped open the back door and helped me in. He then got in the driver's seat, started the engine, and pulled out from our parking spot.

"Where are we going? Where are Everett and Dean?" I asked rapidly, trying to buckle myself.

"Picking them up now." His gaze remained focused on the windshield as we pulled up to the alley and he rolled his window down. "Let's fucking move!" he screamed out the window to the guys, who were still hammering the twins to the pavement. Everett looked up and then started making his way to our car. Dean was still hunched over his twin, whispering something to him before kicking his side and taking off in a jog toward us. Both Everett's and Dean's clothes were caked in the blood that was from the damage they'd caused to the twins' faces. Everett took his seat on the passenger side, and Dean slid in beside me. Dean was breathing heavily. He reached for me, cupping my face in his hands.

"Are you okay, doll? Did they hurt you?" He examined my body, face, wrists, and hands.

"I'm fine. I'm fine." My voice was shaky, and it took all I had not to burst into tears from sheer panic. I had almost been kidnapped again. I looked over to Dean and saw how much blood he was covered in. His shirt was drenched, and his knuckles were cut and bloody. I took his hands in mine, turning them over and over.

"Are you guys okay?" Through the rearview mirror, I looked at each one of them—Dean, then Everett, and then Colson. Silence filled the vehicle. No one answered me as the adrenaline from what had just occurred started to dissipate. I let Dean's hand go and placed my own on my thighs. My hands were trembling as well as my body. There was a tightness in my chest that caused me to lean forward. They saved me, again. They did what they had said they would and protected me from being taken. A tear slid down my face, and I quickly wiped it away before anyone noticed. I lifted my head, not looking at any of them, and with a shaky voice said, "Thank you. You guys saved me again." That was all I could say before

I completely fell apart. Dean pulled me into his chest, holding me close as tears rushed from my eyes. My breathing was so rapid that I thought I might pass out. Everett crawled into the back seat with us and pulled my legs onto his lap. Lying across two of the men who had just saved me, I could feel some of the blood that coated them rub off on me. They let me cry. Both of them were rubbing soothing shapes on my skin.

After about fifteen minutes, I was starting to calm down a bit. My breathing returned to normal, and only a few remaining tears escaped my eyes. I lay there still, allowing the comfort of Everett and Dean to ease my panic. I let the sound of Dean's heartbeat soothe me to sleep; my body still stretched across them both.

CHAPTER 18

SLOAN

The sound of Everett's voice gently awoke me.

"Wake up, love. We're home."

I let go of Dean's shirt and hadn't realized I was gripping it. Patting his shirt down to get rid of the stiff handprints I'd created, I apologized.

"Don't apologize, Sloan. It's us that need to apologize. We shouldn't have let this happen tonight. We didn't keep you safe, like we promised." Dean's voice was dark, sounding furious as he looked down at me with sad eyes. He brushed a loose strand of my hair behind my ear before helping me up and out of the car, right into Everett's waiting arms as he helped me stand on shaky legs. With his hand, he cupped my face and wiped away a lingering tear from my cheek with his thumb. He tilted his head toward the door and placed his hand on the small of my back, leading me through the doorway.

We all walked in silence as we made our way to the kitchen together. Colson was first in the room, cracking open four beers and placing them on the island. Everett and I entered next, each of us grabbing a beer as well. Dean came in last, his heavy boots echoing on the tile as he entered. He held his beer and tilted it back, emptying the entire contents in one single gulp. I sipped mine slowly, as did the others. Once finished, he slammed his bottle on the island surface, making me jump from the loud noise.

"I told you it was a bad idea to go out! She could have been fucking killed!" Dean's voice was loud and hoarse. The other two looked at him, appearing equally as angry at the situation. All three of their eyes filled with fire as they exchanged glares.

"This was my fault. I shouldn't have risked it." Everett's voice was even and calm. His facial expression didn't match his tone. He looked enraged. His cheeks were turning a slight red, and beads of sweat slowly started forming on his forehead.

"I won't be making that mistake again." Everett tilted his bottle, finishing the last bit of beer.

"We couldn't have known the twins would show up. I mean, how the fuck did they know we would be there? Unless they were tipped off," Colson finally spoke. Dean's eyes snapped to Colson, and I could see his fury increase.

"Thank you." My voice was low as I held my head down. They were fighting because of me. If I weren't their little pet to keep safe, this wouldn't have happened. All heads turned to me while I slowly lifted my head from the floor. I scanned their faces one at a time. All three faces, unreadable. "I'm going to take a shower," I announced to the room. Before heading out of the kitchen, I walked up to Dean. I gave him a hug and thanked him. I did the same to Colson and then finally Everett. I thanked them all for saving me, not once but twice now. With that, I turned on my heels and left them all standing in the kitchen. I made it to the top of the stairs before I heard Colson call out for me.

"Sloan, are you okay? Do you need my help?" Colson's voice was soft and soothing. He sounded genuinely concerned for my well-being. I turned to look at him and gave him a gentle smile.

"You've helped me more in these past few days than anyone else in my life. I'm okay. I'm just going to shower and call it a night."

He smiled before he took two steps at a time, until he was standing right in front of me. Looking down at me, he brushed a loose strand of my hair behind my ear.

"I will always be here to help, gorgeous." He kissed the top of my forehead in the most tender way, and my body released all the tension I was holding on to. Releasing my face, he gave me one last smile, which melted my insides, before turning and letting me continue to my room.

"Just call for me if you need anything," he said

over his shoulder before stepping off the last step and entering back into the kitchen.

These men were starting to have a hold on me that was unlike anything I had ever felt before. Although they were all different in their own ways, they each showed they genuinely cared for me. Tonight, being a perfect example. They came for me, again. They saved me, again. These three men had done more for me in the few days I'd known them than my family had my entire life. Being in their presence left me feeling wanted, cared for, and safe. I admit it, I'm falling for all three of them.

CHAPTER 19

SLOAN

I followed the hallway until I reached my room and pushed the door open. I headed straight for the bathroom, not even closing the door behind me. Fuck. I couldn't even recognize the girl staring back at me in the mirror. I was covered in the dried, brown blood that had covered Dean and Everett. My hair was a total mess of knots, and more dried blood was slicked to the side of my head. I turned on the shower faucet to a scalding temperature, determined to get all this chaos washed off my skin. I stripped and pushed my clothes to the bathroom corner and turned to face the mirror once again.

I stared at the girl in the mirror for a long while. I was almost kidnapped again. I was picked up, tied up, and thrown in the back of a vehicle as if I was nothing. I was completely helpless, unable to defend myself or fight my captors. Looking at myself now, I felt utterly weak. I felt defenseless, a damsel in distress who couldn't protect herself in the slightest way.

How had I let myself become so fragile? I slammed my hands on the vanity, anger filling my veins as I let out a grunt of frustration.

"Are you okay, love?" A soft voice asked from outside my bathroom. I straightened up, rushing to grab a towel and wrap myself up before anyone could see me naked.

"Yes, yes, I'm fine. Just thought I saw a bug, that's all." I lied to whoever it was. I turned toward the door as Everett stepped into view and rested his shoulder on the doorframe. With his arms crossed, he gave me a knowing look.

"It's okay not to be okay," he said, his gaze locked on me. I didn't know what to say at that. I just stared back, trying not to break and show anymore weakness than I already had. When the silence became too much, he made his way over to me. Without breaking eye contact, he lifted my hands in his and squeezed them tight.

"Then why are you trembling, Sloan?" I had no idea I was trembling up until now. Looking down at my hands, I saw that they were visibly shaking. Blood was caked on my skin. I dropped my hands from his and turned on the sink to wash off the blood.

"Here, let me help you." Everett reached over to grab my hands once again and started rubbing a washcloth over my hands. Watching the blood run down the sink, I shuddered under his touch. His hands were full of calluses, but his touch was gentle as he carefully wiped the blood, cleaning my skin.

"There, all clean. Now time to get the blood out of your hair." He looked down at me as if he was waiting for me to do something. I held my towel as he lifted his eyebrows at me. "Well, are you going to get in the shower or not?" His question was playful as he gestured to the shower.

"Uhm, are you going to leave?" He let out a small chuckle as he started pulling his shirt over his head with one hand. Why was that so hot when men did that?

"I have a lot of blood on me too. I also need to shower. Is that okay with you?" He gave me a devilish grin before unbuttoning his pants and letting them drop to the floor. Holy fuck! This man was gorgeous. His abs flexed as he moved. His whole body was covered in tattoos—some even dipping below his waistband—and I wanted to see more. He didn't wait for my answer. He just dropped his boxers and opened the glass shower door, stepping in.

"I think I need your help getting some of this blood off. Do you mind?" His head was under the water as it cascaded down his muscular body. Staring at him through the glass, I swallowed hard. Trying to think of anything other than the fact that this insanely hot man was in my shower—I mean his shower.

"Well, love, can you help me?"

I hesitated just a moment more and decided I

needed to get this blood off my body immediately. I dropped my towel, opened the shower door, and stepped in slowly. Standing behind Everett, I admired his tattooed back. They were all so beautiful and incredibly well done. I reached up and traced my finger along the lines that intertwined and overlapped each other. He shivered at my touch and turned around to face me. He had rinsed most of the blood off himself; only some remained in his hair.

"Finally decided to join me, huh?" It wasn't a question but rather a statement. His eyes were full of sin as they roamed my body. Stepping closer to me, he brushed my hair back from my face.

"I'm so sorry for tonight. That should have never happened. I could have prevented everything." His words were full of sadness and anger as he peered into my eyes.

"It's fine. I shouldn't have gone to the restroom alone. That was a stupid mistake." I couldn't look at him in the eye, just looked down as I watched more blood-stained water swirl down the drain. He lifted my chin, so we were face-to-face.

"None of this is your fault, love. We have to do better by you. You don't deserve any of this." I closed my eyes as I let the water run down my face and took in his words. "I told you I would never do anything without your consent, but right now, I want to kiss you so fucking bad." My core tightened, and my pussy throbbed at his words. "I've wanted to kiss those lips every day since the first time at Stone

Fortress." His fingers brushed along my bottom lip. I clenched my thighs together as his other hand snaked around to my lower back.

"I won't do anything you don't want me to. You're in charge here." His hands stopped on my lower back, while his other hand still cupped my face. He stayed there waiting for me to make the next move. I couldn't fight the butterflies that were raging war in my stomach any longer. I, too, wanted to kiss him again after that night. Fuck it.

I lifted to my tiptoes as our lips met in a bruising kiss. He reached around to my neck and held me tighter to his body. Our teeth clicked together as our tongues explored each other's mouths. With our bodies pinned together, I could feel his length harden against my stomach. He pushed my body against the cold tile as he lifted both my arms above my head.

"Fuck," he moaned against my mouth. He was still holding my arms above my head with one hand as the other began tweaking and squeezing my breasts, causing me to arch into his touch. A pathetic moan escaped my mouth as his hand ventured lower and found my now aching pussy. Finding my clit, he slowly—and I mean painfully slow—started making small, circular motions. My knees began to shake as his mouth left mine, and he started nipping my earlobe and then started kissing down my neck.

"Everett," I moaned as he sped up his fingers and started playing my clit like a symphony orchestra. My body slumped as his fingers brought me to the edge of a bone-shattering orgasm. Just before I was about to reach my climax, he stopped and brought his now erect cock to my entrance.

"No, don't stop, please," I pleaded, still trying to chase my climax that was slowly disappearing. He just let out a devilish laugh as he lined up his cock and slammed into my cunt. I gasped at the pain of his enormous size, but also secretly loved the pain. My pussy stretched, accommodating his girth as he slowly withdrew and slammed into me again.

Once he was fully inside of me, he tilted his head down and kissed me hard enough to leave bruises. Holding our kiss, he started setting a pace that quickly had me chasing down my orgasm again. He released my arms from above my head, and I wrapped my arms around his neck, holding on for dear life. He grabbed my ass, lifting me off my feet and pressing me harder into the tile. His cock sunk even deeper inside my pussy and, with this new position, had me shaking as my climax surged through my body, making me scream out in pleasure.

"Atta girl." His voice was a breathy moan as he soon found his release a few thrusts later. He filled me with his cum while his abdomen flexed, his cock still inside me twitching as he rode out his own release.

We just stayed there for a moment—our breathing heavy. He rested his forehead against mine as he slowly lowered me back to my feet, his cock slowly slipping from my pussy. Still holding on to my waist, we let the water spray across our naked bodies. Once we were able to control our breathing, Everett reached for the soap, squeezing a sizeable amount on the washcloth. Rubbing the soap into a lather, he looked down at me.

"Turn around, love, let me wash this off you."

I did as he said. He gently washed across my shoulders, down my back, and up and down my legs. He then spun me around and did the same to my chest, spending an extra amount of time on my breasts. His touch was intoxicating. Every gentle sweep and rub of his hand had my core burning once again. I was already thirsting for round two by the time he was done rinsing me off.

He washed my hair next, making sure all the blood was rinsed thoroughly from my thick blonde hair. Turning off the shower, he reached for a towel outside the glass door and wrapped it over my shoulders. As he did so, he kissed my shoulder gently and pulled my hair over the top of my towel.

"All clean, love."

I turned toward him. "Thank you, Everett." Reaching up onto my tiptoes, I leaned in and gave him one more kiss.

CHAPTER 20

SLOAN

After we finished showering, Everett walked me to my bed and ushered me to sit down. He went back into the bathroom and retrieved a brush. He then sat on the bed behind me and started brushing out my long hair so tenderly that I thought he would never get the tangles out. We just sat in silence as he continued to brush through my blonde hair, causing goosebumps to prickle my skin from the sensation of him brushing my hair. I closed my eyes and allowed him to ease the tangles free from my blood-free hair.

"No one's ever brushed my hair for me before." I admitted to him. He stopped brushing for a moment, taking in my words, and slowly started to brush the last remaining tangles free. Placing the brush beside us, he spun my body around so we were facing each other. He pushed my hair behind my ear and leaned in to kiss my forehead, keeping his warm lips against my skin for a long moment.

"Sloan, who's hurt you? Tell me everyone who's ever done you wrong, and I will take care of them myself." He was serious, his words a promise as he spoke while still resting against my forehead.

I closed my eyes as flashes of my past soared through my brain, causing my body to tense against his touch. He sensed my pain as he pulled me into his embrace.

"Don't worry. You're safe with us now. No one will ever hurt you again," he whispered in my ear, and it was at that moment I knew. I could trust him. I could trust all three of them.

After a long while, Everett pulled down my sheets, picked me up, and laid me in my bed before removing my towel and pulling up the comforter, covering my naked body. He leaned in and kissed me softly and said, "Get some rest." He then turned and started toward my door. I sat straight up in protest.

"Please, don't leave me tonight." My words were pleading as he turned to look at me, still in his own towel that was draped so low that I was surprised it was still holding on. He gave me a small smile before turning back around and making his way to the other side of my bed.

"Of course, love." He pulled off his towel, exposing his muscular body and climbed in next to me. I inched my way closer to him as he opened his arms to me. I lay against his chest, his arms holding me tight as our naked bodies pressed firmly together.

It didn't take long for me to fall into a deep sleep. The sound of his heart beating lulled me to sleep, while my body released the tension it had been holding. Everett stayed with me, making me feel safe, as his huge arms covered my small frame.

I awoke to the sound of people talking outside my bedroom door. I stretched my body, noticing Everett was gone. The spot on the bed where he'd been sleeping still felt warm, so he must have just left. Sitting up in bed, I held the sheets to my chest and tried to listen to the conversation going on in the hallway. Whoever it was sounded pissed.

"It was Arno's guys from last night, the twins."

It sounded a lot like Colson who was speaking.

"I'll fucking kill him and the twins," Everett snarled, venom coursing through his words.

"Get in line, bro," Dean chimed in, his voice deep and threaded with devilish promise. "You should have let me finish them last night and be done with it, send Arno a message," he continued. There was a brief silence as I got up and slowly tiptoed my way to the door to listen further.

"We need to take care of this, Everett. Arno is getting too damn ballsy for his own good. He needs to remember who the fuck he's dealing with." Colson's voice was low but audible through the door.

"Agreed," Dean replied.

"Get with Drew, and find out where Arno is staying. We'll pay him a visit tonight. It's about time this fucker knows who we are."

"Fuck yes," one of them said.

I opened the door, and all three guys stared down at me. They were shirtless, all three of them looking as though they had just rolled out of bed. Damn, they were gorgeous. If I didn't know any better, I would think they were brothers, all three covered in tattoos, not an inch of spare skin left. I forgot I was naked until their eyes roamed over my barely covered body. I had grabbed the sheet from the bed and wrapped myself up just enough to conceal the goods. Even with the sheet, I felt way too exposed.

"Good morning, guys." I yawned through my words.

"Fuck me. Good morning, gorgeous." Colson moaned as his eyes trailed up and down my body. Everett slapped the back of his head, causing Colson to bark in protest.

"What the fuck, bro?"

"Sorry we woke you, doll," Dean said as he leaned against the wall beside me, arms crossed over his impressively large chest.

I'm going to need a very cold shower this morning. I clenched my thighs together while my core began heating from just looking at these half-naked gods of men standing in front of me.

"You hungry?" Everett asked, standing in front of me in nothing but his boxers. I licked my bottom lip, remembering exactly what was beneath them, before I answered.

"Starving actually."

"I'll start on breakfast. Take your time and meet us downstairs."

"Or you can come to breakfast in the sheet. I wouldn't mind." Colson's voice was playful as he smiled down at me, his eyes revealing just how hungry he was.

I couldn't help the look I gave in return, my eyes giving away just how hungry I was for all three of them as well. I gave him a sly wink before I turned to head to my bathroom and wash up for the day.

CHAPTER 21

SLOAN

I didn't bother taking a shower, since I had already last night. I quickly dressed and threw my hair in a messy bun before heading to the kitchen. I practically ran with how hungry I was. Making it halfway down the stairs, I was invaded by the sweet smell of waffles and cinnamon. Smiling wide, I walked through the archway of the kitchen, just in time for Everett to place the plate holding a waffle on the island in front of an empty barstool.

"That smells amazing," I said, making my way to the island and taking the empty barstool right next to Dean.

"Good, I haven't cooked in a long time so hopefully these are good," Everett admitted, looking a little worried as he pushed the plate in front of me and set a small glass pitcher of syrup on the island beside me.

"I'm sure they are delicious." I gave him a reas-suring smile as I picked up my fork and started to cut into the fluffy waffle. I took a bite and almost died right there in their kitchen. My taste buds had never tasted something so decadent and delicious, ever.

"They are amazing, thank you!" I looked up to see all three guys staring at me while I continued to shovel waffles into my mouth.

"Good. She needed to eat something. She's getting smaller and smaller every time I look at her," Colson said from over his coffee mug. He was standing at the end of the island, still shirtless, and I had to swallow hard to keep from drooling over his impressively toned torso. Jesus, save me from my dirty thoughts that were now taking hold of my brain.

I looked away quickly before anyone could notice how creepy I was being, staring at his chest. I took another bite, and then I looked down at my plate and was shocked to see that the waffle had disappeared. I was hungrier than I had thought. Just then Dean's hand rested on mine. I looked up at his face, his emotions unreadable.

"Slow down, or you're going to make yourself sick," he said to me before slowly removing his hand from mine. Slightly embarrassed, I set my fork down and pulled my hand from his. Colson placed a mug of freshly brewed coffee in front of me. Its silky aroma filled my senses. Hell yes.

"Here you are, gorgeous," Colson said as smug as ever while smiling down at me and appearing at my side. He was standing so close that I could feel his heat radiating off his exposed chest. I took the mug, sipping the coffee slowly. I could get used to waking up like this. Three gorgeous men making me waffles and coffee; life couldn't get better than this.

"You guys sure know how to spoil a girl."

Colson chuckled at my comment and leaned in to kiss the top of my head. "You're worth spoiling," he said as he propped up on the counter to my side, still sipping his own coffee. While I had all three of them together, I wanted to ask them about the conversation they'd had earlier about Arno.

"What did you guys mean when you said you were going to take care of Arno?" No better way to ask than to just come right out with it. Right? The room went silent for a moment, the guys frozen in place.

"He needs to be reminded that we are not to be fucked with, and you are off-limits indefinitely," Dean spoke, not making eye contact with me but just continuing to sip his coffee. I just stared at the side of his beautiful face, remembering the moment we had yesterday before I got into the pool.

Dean was a mystery to me. First, he was all dark and standoffish with me, acting as though he hated my presence. Then he turned into this guy who understood the pain I'd felt my whole life, as if he, too, had experienced the same. The Dean in the kitchen right now was the dark and mysterious Dean. The one I wanted to know more about. I wanted to know the dark and terrible things that created the man who sat beside me. I felt connected to him in a disturbing way, as if he were the only other person who had experienced the same torture and torment I had. There was a dark shadow that swept around him, and as much as he wanted to let go of it, it was holding on to him, like a plague that has no cure. I understood that shadow, since I had my very own as well.

"What they did to you last night was inexcusable. Their actions cannot go unnoticed, and they will pay the consequences of trying to take what's ours." Everett's tone was stern. What did he mean by that?

"I'm yours?" My voice was small, and I was starting to get pissed at myself for how pitiful I was starting to sound around these guys. I needed to toughen the fuck up. Everett didn't respond right away. He just gave me a look that was hard to read. He didn't look mad or annoyed, but I wasn't sure what his reaction was going to be at my comment.

"Yes, for the time being. Your safety is our top priority. We got you into this mess, and we are going to make sure you are safe before letting you leave."

I wasn't sure if I should be mad that he'd just told me I was his property or relieved that the three of them were going to protect me from any further kidnapping attempts. I was silent for a moment, not knowing what to say back.

"Just think of us as your roommates. How does that sound?" Colson asked in his usual joking tone.

He was fast becoming the one I tagged the "jokester" of this trio, and I liked it. Each one similar, but so incredibly different at the same time. Dean chuckled at Colson's comment, but didn't say anything else. I looked to Everett, his sexy smile spreading across his face.

"I guess you could call it that," Everett replied to Colson, turning and pouring himself more coffee. Just then Everett's phone rang, and he stepped out of the kitchen for a moment, leaving the three of us together.

"So, sweetheart, what would you like to do today?" Colson hopped off the counter and walked to the sink to dispose of his mug. I sat there, still squeezing my mug in my hands and leaning back on the barstool. I really had no idea what to do. I was so used to being on my own and working all the time to make ends meet that I really had no time for anything else.

"Uhm, I don't know." Taking the last sip of my coffee, I set the mug on the island and looked between the guys. Both were looking at me intently now.

"What do you normally do for fun?" Dean asked in his deep, husky voice.

"I don't really know. I used to work all the time just to make enough money to pay for my room at the hostel. I never really had free time." My cheeks heated as they stared at me in disbelief.

"You're telling me a girl like you never made time

for herself to just let loose and have fun?" Colson sounded shocked at my answer.

"I like to swim," I finally admitted, trying to make myself not sound so pathetic.

"She's damn good at it too." Dean's voice was low as if he didn't mean to say that out loud. Had he been watching me swim the other day? I guess he kind of had to. The glass doors in the living room did lead to the pool. I gave him a curious look, his face not giving anything away.

"So little minnow, you like to swim, huh? I have to say I am pretty fond of swimming myself," Colson said proudly as he sat up a bit straighter. Dean let out a short huff.

"Since when is swimming your new favorite activity, asshole?" Dean asked, with sarcasm laced between every word.

"I have always liked swimming. I just enjoy it a lot more now that we have a new roommate who I can share my passions with." Colson smiled ear to ear as he responded to Dean, before turning his charming smile to me.

I smiled as the banter between the two continued. I was starting to enjoy the company these three men gave me. I had never been the outgoing type, or the talking type for that matter. Having these three around, I was beginning to feel like a normal twenty-three-year-old.

As Dean and Colson continued their bickering, I turned my head to see where Everett had disappeared to. Standing from my barstool, I tiptoed out of the kitchen without the guys even noticing I had left. I followed the muffled sound of Everett still on his phone. His voice was all business, and I couldn't quite make out what he was saying. I followed his voice to his office beside the foyer and leaned against the outside of the doorframe to eavesdrop. He sounded annoyed at whoever he was talking to.

"It doesn't take this long to find out where he lives, Drew. He and his guys were able to find our residence as well as follow us to dinner and almost succeed in kidnapping Sloan." His voice was starting to get louder as he spoke to Drew. "You find his location before tonight. This fucker is going to pay for thinking he could mess with us. If he thinks he is the best, he's got another thing coming. Find him, Drew. I want an update before five this evening. The boys and I are going hunting."

Just as I was about to enter the office, a firm hand locked around my waist as my back was pulled into something hard.

"It's not polite to eavesdrop, doll." Dean's voice was a whisper, his breath hot on my neck.

I didn't know what to say. I just leaned into his chest even more, feeling the rise and fall of his breathing. His hand on my waist was like a furnace igniting my skin and causing my brain to short-circuit. I inhaled the scent that was Dean, fresh soap and cologne that had my knees go weak.

"What's wrong? Cat got your tongue?"

I blinked a few times to regain my bearings and turned to face him. He was giving me a sly smile, like he knew what his mere presence did to me. Two could play that game. I took a step closer to him, now having to crane my neck due to his height, but I didn't care. I met his steel-gray eyes as his smile slipped from his face. His eyes narrowed on me like he was trying to read my body language. I placed my hand on his chest before replying, "Just wanted to see what the boss was up to, since it looks like he is the one getting the important phone calls." I patted his chest and started making my way past him, but he grabbed my arm, stopping me.

"He's not the boss. We all have our own roles. You're in a house with three alphas; don't forget that." His eyes were heated, and I knew I had struck a nerve with him.

"Whatever you tell yourself to sleep better at night." I gave him a sheepish smile and tugged my arm from his grasp, leaving him outside the office.

CHAPTER 22

DEAN

Watching her leave me in the hallway, I couldn't help but chuckle inside. She had a smart mouth, a mouth I wanted to explore some more. Smiling to myself I headed into the office to see who had called Everett.

"Who was that, and what did they want?" I asked, getting down to business.

Everett was sprawled out on the chair behind the desk, looking way too annoyed by one call. Brushing his hair back, he sighed. "It was Drew, and he still hasn't pinpointed Arno's location." Everett's tone was full of frustration, and I knew what he was feeling. We were considered the best, but the two most recent incidents with our home and then at Rocco's had the blood in my veins flowing hotter by the day. It was only a matter of time before Arno fucked up, as he usually did, and that's when we would attack.

"What about tonight? If he doesn't find the loca—"

Everett cut me off. "We're still on for tonight. Drew will find him. We can't let another day slip by and allow him to think he's even on the same playing board as us. He started this bullshit, and I intend to finish it." His tone oozed confidence, and I knew without a shadow of a doubt, Arno was about to pay.

"Who stays with the girl tonight?" I asked, genuinely wondering what the fuck we were going to do with her.

"I have a few guys coming to guard the house. I also have Cain and Stone, who have strict orders not to let her out of their sight."

I sat back in the chair directly opposite of Everett. "I'm not too sure she will agree to this. She's starting to come out of her shell and is a whole lot more feisty as the days go by."

"She doesn't have a choice, Dean. It's either this or take the risk of leaving her without protection, and I'm not willing to risk that."

He was right. I, too, didn't feel comfortable leaving her without at least one of us three. Although we had our own security and people we trusted with specific jobs, I never trusted anyone other than my brothers. We'd been through more shit in our lives than any other team to come out of The Shadows.

"Want to draw straws to see who gets the honor of telling her?"

Everett chuckled at my question. "Nah, let's make

Colson tell her. Mr. Charming, himself, will have the best luck of her not losing her shit on us."

Laughing at this, I had to agree. Colson had a way with charming woman, or maybe it was just the way he was able to twist the truth and make them believe it wasn't as big of a deal as they made it out to be.

"Sounds good to me," I replied. I gave him a hard stare as he sat there, swirling a crystal tumbler that was a quarter full of whiskey. I sat up straighter in my chair and leaned my forearms on my knees before asking him, "Did you fuck her last night, bro?"

He didn't answer me. All he gave me was a devilish grin before tipping back the remainder of his whiskey.

I took that as a yes. Lucky bastard.

CHAPTER 23

SLOAN

After telling Colson I loved to swim, he practically yelled at me to go get my swimsuit on and meet him by the pool. I never said no to a good swim opportunity, so I did as I was told and ran upstairs, skipping every other step. After changing into my suit, I grabbed a towel and headed for the backyard. Colson was already waiting for me, sitting on the edge of the pool with his legs dangling in the water. He was leaning back on his hands with only his swimsuit on, looking like a fucking *GQ* model.

Colson was definitely the most ripped of the guys. Since all three had a tendency of going shirtless, I knew. His abs glistened in the afternoon sun, and water slowly dripped down his obnoxiously defined abs. He was already wet from being in the pool, but I wasn't complaining. As soon as he noticed me, he brushed back his blond, wet hair with both hands, slicking it back away from his face. Damn, that was sexy.

"There you are, sweetheart. Took you long enough. I thought you ditched me."

Smiling to myself, I was secretly starting to love the nicknames each guy had for me. I placed my towel across one of the lounge chairs and made my way to the stairs of the pool. The air was chilly, and I knew the pool was warm, so I didn't hesitate stepping right in and submerging my entire body with one swift motion. Pushing off the bottom of the pool, I re-emerged, brushing my own hair back. Opening my eyes, I let out a small yelp as Colson was standing directly in front of me.

"Jesus, I didn't see you get back in," I admitted, wiping down my face and removing excess water. He just chuckled his sexy laugh and dipped back under the water, swimming to the deep end. I watched the muscles in his back as he broke the water's surface and waded in the water. Turning around, he caught me staring and gave me a wink. I rolled my eyes, playing off that I wasn't in fact staring at his incredibly hard body.

I was forming a connection with each of them. Colson definitely being the most playful, Dean being the most mysterious—and I loved pushing his buttons—and Everett... Well, he was the most grounded, and he made me feel safe and wanted—feelings I have never felt in my young existence.

"Let's play a game," Colson said, smiling back at

me as I slowly started swimming his way. I couldn't remember the last time I played a game, so of course I agreed.

"Okay, what game then?" I asked, grabbing the edge of the pool and dipping my hair back in the water.

"Truth or dare?"

I turned my head to face him, and the smile he was displaying was that of a high school boy's. I laughed at him. "Fine, but only because I haven't played that game since I was like ten."

He hopped out of the pool and propped himself on the edge before saying, "Perfect. Okay, gorgeous, you first."

I had a feeling he would say dare, so I pondered what I would make him do. "Okay, truth or dare, Colson?"

He didn't even think about his answer. "Truth."

Not what I was expecting but all right. I turned my back to the edge of the pool and stretched my arms behind me so that I could hold on. I looked at him for a moment, thinking about what I wanted to know about him.

"Okay then, where are you originally from, because let's be honest, you don't sound like you're from England?" There was a hint of something else in his drawl, and I had grown curious as to where he was from. He laughed and looked down at his hands as if the answer were in his palms.

"I was born in Detroit, Michigan, actually. My

mother was American, and after I was born, my father relocated us here. So yes, the accent is real, but I also grew up with my mother and her American accent. I guess I took after both of my parents, but my American accent shines through, and that's what you're stuck with, my dear." He smiled at me. "All right, my turn. Truth or dare?"

I was being a coward and didn't want to be the first one to choose dare, so I went with truth. He nodded and then looked to the sky, pondering his question. Suddenly he looked toward me and clapped his hands. "Okay, got one. Did you fuck Everett last night?"

My jaw dropped and my cheeks heated. The embarrassment was displayed right on my face. I was never the one that could hide my emotions, so my sudden embarrassment was all the answer he needed.

"I knew it! That lucky fucker." Colson practically yelled. He was laughing as he leaned his head back. He then pushed off the edge of the pool and hopped back in the pool. He swam underwater toward me and then popped up right in front of me. He jerked his head to the side, spraying me with the water that was soaking his hair.

"Hey, watch it!" I yelled, wiping the water from my face. He just laughed, making me laugh too. As soon as I did, he jerked his head toward me, staring right into my eyes.

"I haven't heard you laugh that hard before."

I just smiled and looked down to the water.

"It's adorable, don't hide it." He swam to my side and rested his back against the edge. He placed his arms outside of the pool against the edge to hold himself up as I was doing and said, "Okay, your turn again."

"Truth or dare, Colson?"

"Truth." Again, he surprised me with truth. He seemed like the guy who would always choose dare to impress the ladies, but he had me fooled.

"Uhm, okay, I got one. What's The Shadows?"

He gave me a hard look, almost like he was debating on telling me at all. He brushed his long hair back again, and I quickly looked away because that simple move had my core burning for him. He sighed and then turned to me. "I shouldn't be telling you any of this, hell, you shouldn't even know what The Shadows is. Fuck it." He sighed again before submerging only his mouth for a moment. "*We* are The Shadows, Sloan. That's what we are called, or the organization we work for is. We have been raised, hell, we were bred for this type of work. Since we were kids, the three of us were thrown into this life and taught to be … " He hesitated before continuing, like it was physically hurting him to tell me anymore.

"You don't have to tell me if you don't want to," I said, seeing how much this question was affecting him.

He just shook his head and continued. "It's fine. Anyway, the three of us grew up in a training camp— if you will—that taught us every way to kill a person without being caught. We learned to fight, to work as a unit, to kill first and ask questions later. We kill people who are assigned to us, people in this world who don't deserve to walk the face of the Earth. They are bad people, Sloan, and when we are sent a target, we eliminate them, no questions asked. So, when we got you as a target, but were instructed to deliver you rather than kill you, we knew something was off. Again, we did our job, but the moment we saw that you were being delivered to Stone Fortress, the three of us knew we were going to get you back." He sighed, pushing off the edge of the pool and wading in front of me. "Something has changed within the organization, especially if they are getting in the business of sex trafficking. That's not who we are, and we intend to put a stop to it."

My heart was pounding, and I could feel the sting of tears filling my eyes. Colson must have noticed because instead of saying anything, he just grabbed my arms and pulled me into his embrace. I didn't fight him, since even though they were the ones who had taken me, they were also the ones who had fought tooth and nail to protect me. They had kept their word in protecting me from their mistake, and I was starting to feel like they were my only hope of surviving—surviving whatever the hell my current situation was. I wrapped my arms around his neck and allowed him to hold me afloat as he bounced us in the water.

We stayed like that for a long moment. His

embrace was soothing, and he started drawing designs with his finger along my lower back. I had always been the girl to protect myself and rely on nobody, but these guys were starting to have a hold on me. A hold that allowed me to slowly lower my walls and let them into the darkness that was Sloan. Never in my life had another soul guarded me as these three had in the last few days.

I held on to him tighter as he began to slowly spin us around.

"Thank you," I whispered in his ear.

"For what, sweetheart?"

I hesitated a moment, feeling the water swirl around us as he continued to spin.

"For caring."

He pulled away from me to look at my face. He placed his hand under my chin, our eyes locked on one another. My stomach was in knots as I took in his beauty, his gentleness, his touch. This was Colson, the sweetest out of the three. He was soft and charming, everything I needed in this moment. His thumb brushed my lower lip, and I closed my eyes at the sensation. A shiver ran straight down my spine at his touch.

Then his lips softly met mine, and I pushed into his embrace. Wrapping my legs around his torso, I was met by the sudden stiffness of his cock pressing against my aching core. I couldn't remember when we stopped spinning; I just felt the chill of the edge of the pool as his chest pushed into mine a little harder.

His tongue forced my lips apart, and I welcomed him as my tongue collided with his.

A soft moan slipped from my mouth as his hand caressed my breast. He squeezed just hard enough for me to feel the pain of pleasure, but not hard enough to make me stop him. His hand slid down my stomach and slowly dipped into my bikini bottoms.

The moment he found my clit, I could have come on his fingers right then. His thumb started making circular motions on my clit, and I had to break from our kiss to let out a heavy breath.

His lips traveled from my neck to just below my ear, and he started kissing me some more. I released one of my hands from his neck and raked it down his chest and abs as my fingers moved over every dip and crevice of his delicious muscles. As I reached the top of his shorts, he thrusted a finger inside me, making me yell out.

"You like that, baby girl?" This was not a question but rather a statement. I couldn't form words, just nodded my approval. My hand slipped slowly inside his shorts and found his fully erect cock waiting for my eager hand. I wrapped my hand around his base and was shocked to learn I couldn't fully grasp him— he was too big.

"Something wrong?"

"No nothing at all," I lied, now imagining what he was going to feel like inside me. I started pumping him slowly, before picking up my pace.

"Fuck," he moaned in my ear as he introduced

another finger in my tight pussy. I could feel my orgasm building within, and once he thrusted a third finger inside me, I was seeing stars. I came so hard, my pussy clenching tight around his fingers as he kept them inside me and I rode out my orgasm.

Panting hard, I pulled his shorts down, freeing his enormous cock. I wanted him inside me, and now. He caught on quick, because he pulled out his fingers and grabbed the sides of my suit bottoms, pulling them down. Helping me to step out of them, he then threw them over his shoulder as he cupped my ass with both his hands. Pulling me slightly out of the water, he lined his cock up with my entrance and slowly pushed his head inside me.

"Colson," I moaned, tilting my head back.

"You okay, sweetheart?" he asked, making sure he wasn't hurting me.

"Yes, fuck, yes, give me more," I demanded, and those were all the instructions he needed. He thrusted inside of me so hard, I gasped at how deep he pushed.

Colson was gifted, very truly gifted. He pulled out slowly and pushed in again, letting out his own moan of pleasure. He set a pace, and I could feel another orgasm building within me. He released one of my ass cheeks and snaked his hand between us, finding my throbbing clit once more. It didn't take long before he had me moaning through a second orgasm, as I squeezed my legs around his waist and my pussy clenched around his cock. He followed behind me with his own release, pushing his cock so far inside me I thought I might come again. He filled me up with his cum while he rested his forehead against mine.

We stayed like that with him still inside me until I felt his dick twitch as his orgasm slowly dissipated. His lips found mine again. My legs were trembling, and I couldn't have been more thankful that we were in the water. I doubted my legs would be able to hold me up after that incredible sex.

"Well, that was entertaining," Dean's husky voice broke our tranquility, and I jerked my head to the side. There he was, sitting back in the lounge chair with his arms folded behind his head and legs crossed in front of him.

How long had he been watching?

"Enjoy the show, bro," Colson said playfully as he reached behind himself and grabbed my floating bottoms, handing them to me. Colson looked back toward me, giving me a smile.

"Don't mind him; he has a thing for watching." He shot me a wink. I quickly stepped into my suit bottoms and swam to the stairs of the pool. Dean watched me the whole way, his gaze hot on my skin.

"Everett needs to talk to you, Colson, so put your dick away." Dean sat up from his chair, pulling his legs to the side and resting his forearms on his knees.

Colson grabbed his towel and proceeded to walk inside, but not before he looked back in my direction, blowing me a kiss. I couldn't help the smile that crept across my face. He was indeed a charmer and I loved it. Dean stood from where he was sitting and made his way over to me. Although I had just had the most fulfilling sex, the butterflies in my stomach instantly awoke at his presence, and I had to swallow hard. Once again, I couldn't keep my raging attraction to just one of them. I wanted them all. *Was I digging my own grave? What would they each think of me? I wondered what Everett would say now that I'd fucked him and Colson? Damn it, Sloan.*

Reaching a hand to my face, he cupped my chin and tilted my face to his.

"I like the sounds you make, doll, especially when there's a dick inside you." Then he walked away.

CHAPTER 24

COLSON

"I have to tell her! What the fuck, man, why not you or Dean for that matter?"

I couldn't believe these cowards were going to make me tell Sloan she was to be guarded by men she didn't know, and we were going to kill some more people.

"You're the smoothest one, Colson. Plus, after what you both just did in the pool, I'd say she is pretty fond of you." Everett's laugh filled the office, just in time for Dean to come strolling in.

"Don't act like you didn't fuck her last night, too, bro," I barked at him.

Dean was laughing behind me. I shot him a glare. He was standing all stoic and shit, leaning against the doorframe with his arms crossed as usual.

"Dude, you know you're the most charming out of the three of us. You should feel honored you were chosen." Dean's tone was sarcastic as fuck. He clicked his tongue ring against his teeth.

"Yeah, but you two assholes chose without me present, so that left me with no say in the matter." I tried to sound angry, but in all reality, I was glad I was not present, or I wouldn't have had fun with Sloan in the pool.

"Suck it up, cupcake. You've been chosen, so man up, turn on the charm, and drop the bomb easily."

I leaned back and punched Dean in the shoulder for that, but he just shook me off and laughed.

Leaving the office, I set out to find Sloan. She was halfway up the stairs, when I called after her, "Hey, Sloan, can I talk to you a second?"

She didn't reply, just nodded. She turned and sat on the step she was currently at, and I made my way to her. She was wrapped in her towel, still a little wet from the pool, a small puddle forming beneath her feet on the step. I sat close to her, wrapping my arm around her shoulders and pulling her into me. She snuggled into my shoulder, and I couldn't help kissing the top of her head.

"You're amazing. Has anyone ever told you that?" I asked, leaning my head on top of hers.

She huffed a small sound. "Never." Her voice was small, laced with a bit of sadness.

"You sure haven't been around the right people then, sweetheart."

"Never in my twenty-three years."

At that comment, I truly wanted to inflict serious

pain on every person who'd ever wronged her. But all I said was "I'll fix that."

We sat there for a long while as I worked up the courage to tell her the plans for this evening. I didn't want to be another person to hurt her in her life. Hell, I never wanted her to hurt ever again. I needed to choose my words carefully, so she would know this was how we were protecting her. I trusted our guys to guard her while we were handling business—not as much as I trusted Dean and Everett—but enough to leave her alone with them for a few hours.

"Sloan," I said cautiously, "the guys and I have to leave this evening to handle a few things to ensure your safety. We have a few guys coming to watch the house while we are away. No need to worry, though. It's our security team. You will be 100 percent protected with them."

She leaned back and stared at me a while, not responding. I couldn't read her face, but she seemed so calm as she took in my words.

"So, I get to stay with a couple of babysitters while the three of you go do whatever it is you do? Why can't I come with you guys?" Her eyes were piercing as she spoke, leaving a feeling of guilt deep in my gut.

"It won't be safe where we're going; you're much safer here."

Again, she didn't answer right away. She just looked at me with those beautiful crystal-blue eyes.

"I feel safest with you guys," she replied barely above a whisper. This wasn't the answer I was expecting, but I couldn't say I was mad at the fact she only felt her safest with us. We were doing something right at least. I sighed with that response and pulled her in again to kiss her forehead.

I heard the sound of footsteps and looked up to see Dean making his way over to where we sat. I gave him a look that said be gentle, you unsensitive asshole. He must have read my expression because he just gave me a small head nod. He sat down on the step below us, but angled his body sideways so he could see our faces.

"Hey, doll," Dean said in his predatorial voice.

She lifted her head off my shoulder, letting out a small sigh. "Hey, perv."

I couldn't help the laugh that escaped me and apparently neither could Dean because he, too, laughed out loud at that comment.

"Touché," Dean said in between laughs.

As our laughter slowly disappeared, the three of us just sat in silence.

"Your safety, love, is all we are concerned about right now. We will never be putting you in danger. Never again," Everett said as he strolled out of the office with both hands in his pants pockets. We all looked up at him as he continued toward us. He joined Dean on the step below us, propping his arms on his knees. "Listen, the men who tried to take you from us need to be taught a lesson. They need to know they made the biggest fucking mistake of their lives coming after you. I think I speak for the three of us when I say we all care for you, so coming with us tonight is not an option. We can't predict how the night will turn out, and we are not willing to risk your life by having you come with us."

Even though I was indeed the most charming out of us bastards, Everett sure as hell had a way with words when he needed to. I looked to Sloan to try and read how she would interpret Everett's words. She didn't look mad, but rather she looked concerned.

"I'm not mad for not going with you guys, but believe it or not, I care for you three. I'm just worried something will happen to one of you."

Everett gave her a mischievous smile before responding, "Sloan, we are the best of the best. You should be more worried about the other guys."

I gave a laugh in agreement, as did Dean. She tried not to smile, but the grin that pulled at the side of her lip let me know she was okay with this.

"Fine. Who are my babysitters for this evening?" Sloan looked at each one of us, and all we could do was smile back at her. Sloan had a gravitational pull on us, even heartless Dean. The three of us were truly fucked in falling for the same girl.

CHAPTER 25

EVERETT

We piled in my black Range Rover, the safest of our vehicles. I had the windows bulletproofed, just in case. Leaving Sloan at the house felt wrong. Although we needed to handle the issues at hand, I still didn't feel comfortable with her not being with one of us. I gripped the steering wheel hard enough to turn my knuckles white as I pressed the gas pedal harder.

"She'll be fine, bro. Cain and Stone won't let her out of their sight," Dean said from the passenger seat. He adjusted his gun holster, which was attached to his chest, and ensured his guns were cocked and ready. I didn't respond, just kept driving at a speed well over the legal limit.

"They'd better keep their fucking eyes and hands to themselves," Colson commented from the backseat. He was flipping his butterfly knife around in his hand, a habit he'd developed throughout the years.

"Don't worry, cupcake, no one is going to touch your new play toy," Dean replied, looking over his shoulder at Colson.

"Fuck off, bro. Don't act like you haven't tasted her sweet mouth either. I saw the two of you in the kitchen."

I gave Dean a look, not realizing he, too, had made a move on Sloan. Dean didn't reply. He just shifted in his seat, spreading his legs wider.

"Enough you two. Get your heads on straight. No distractions." My tone was serious and hard.

We received Arno's residential location a couple of hours ago from Drew, and we wasted no time. Leaving Sloan with Cain and Stone,

as well as the three other guys who were in charge of guarding the outside perimeter, we loaded up with enough weapons to supply a small army. Arno, the piece of shit, was about to learn not to fuck with us or Sloan anymore.

The rest of the drive was quiet, only the radio played with some heavy metal shit Dean had clicked on. About an hour later, we found Arno's house and passed by, only to stop on the curb roughly a block away. Shutting off the car, I inhaled a deep breath as the blood in my veins began to run hot.

"Dean, you take the east side of the house. Colson and I will take the west. Remember his security cameras have blind spots on the outermost parts of the gates. Stay hidden, I want to keep the element of surprise for these fuckers. Dean, no guns until we've breached the house, understood?" I gave him a hard look, but he just nodded before turning back to his window. Dean was always the most bloodthirsty out of us three. He enjoyed the hunt, but even more he loved the kill. His body count had surpassed Colson's and mine long ago.

"Drew informed me that he had eyes on the twins as well, so expect the three of them tonight." Colson chuckled in the back.

"Good, I want to leave a few more bruises on those fuckers for interrupting our dinner. I didn't even get to try the ravioli." I turned to look at Colson, but he was staring out his window, looking angrier than I had ever seen him. Hey, the kid liked his food; that's for damn sure.

I rubbed my hand down my face and checked both my guns were cocked and secured in my shoulder holsters.

"Fuck, now I'm hungry." Dean leaned his head back, holding his stomach as if he hadn't just eaten dinner an hour ago.

For fuck's sake, we were about to destroy some people, and these two bastards couldn't stop thinking about food. Just as I was about to smack the back of Dean's head, my stomach let out a growl that was loud enough to echo in the car.

"Sounds like we're all hungry." Colson laughed from the backseat.

"Pizza on the way home." I looked between the

guys, and they both shook their heads with approval as smiles curved both of their lips.

"Business first, then food. Now let's stop fucking around and teach some pricks a lesson, shall we?"

We exited the car, all jokes dissipated, as our Shadows' personas switched into place. We were ready.

Walking along the gates of Arno's estate, I gave Dean a look while he continued to the west side of the property. Colson followed close behind me as we took the east side and quietly hopped the fence, avoiding all cameras in sight. Reaching the grass on his property, I pulled a gun from my holster and held it out in front of me. Colson already had his drawn and was searching the grounds while keeping pace with me.

Reaching the side of the house, or mansion rather, we pressed our bodies against the cold stone of the exterior. Walking along the side of the mansion, we approached the corner. I knew from here the cameras would detect us, so I motioned to Colson to take them out. He nodded and twisted his silencer onto the barrel of his gun. He was the best shot out of the three of us. In all the time since I'd known him, I hadn't seen him miss his target, not once.

Crouching on the ground in front of me, he took up his position, angled himself around the corner, and took one shot. Camera was out. Although this would alert Arno something was wrong, we didn't want him thinking someone shot out his camera, plus Colson always brought his silencer with him. That kid was a creature of habit.

Colson gave me a nod, and we continued along the side of the house, reaching Arno's sliding glass doors that led to his concrete patio. We pushed our bodies against the side of the house once more and waited for them to exit the house to inspect the now destroyed camera.

It didn't take long before the glass door slid open and one of the twins stepped outside. A half second later the second twin joined his brother. I lifted my gun, placing it on the temple of one of the guys as Dean did the same to the other. Colson stepped in front, aiming his gun at the two of them.

"Inside, we need to have a little chat." My voice was like venom as it slid between my lips. Both the twins looked rough—still covered in bruises, both eyes blacked out, and one looked as if his nose had been broken and hadn't been set properly. They didn't say a word as they backed into the house, hands by their sides. Backing into the house I heard the faint sound of Arno from another room. Following the twins, I lifted my finger and pressed it to my lips informing them to keep quiet.

"Well, what the fuck happened to the back camera?" Arno turned the corner, entering the large living room that now held three unexpected visitors. Colson now pointed his gun at Arno, with a fucking smile that could kill stretched across his face. "Well, hello, Arno. Nice to see you. How about you take a seat; we have a few things we need to discuss with you and your boys."

Dean approached the twins, removing their pistols that were tucked into both of their jeans and placed them in his own. He then pushed the two onto the couch behind them in a less than gentle way. After he zip tied their hands together as well as their legs, they just glared daggers at Dean as he worked quickly. Colson kept his gun pointed at the two, while I redirected mine to Arno. He was still standing at the entrance of the living room, and took my instructions as suggestions rather than demands.

"I suggest you take a seat, Arno, I'm not against putting a bullet in you just to see what color you bleed."

Narrowing his eyes on me, he slowly made his way to a sofa chair, sitting down and placing his arms on his knees. I pulled the gun that was strapped to his shoulder holster and handed it to Colson, not taking my eyes off him. Arno looked over at his friends, giving them a disgusted look and then back to me.

"To what do I owe the pleasure of your company, gentleman?" Arno couldn't hide the anger boiling up from his chest as he barked the question. The mere smirk he was displaying made me react without thinking. Lifting the butt of my gun, I came down hard across his face.

The audible sound of bones crunching beneath the force had the guys laughing behind me. The pleasure that filled my veins had my lips curling into a devilish smile. Blood erupted from Arno's mouth as his head snapped to the side. A deep growl escaped from his chest, but he made no move to retaliate. Smart man.

"Now that I have your attention, I have a few questions about why your guys felt the need to touch my girl?" I began walking around Arno's chair as I asked the question. A power move I had learned over the years—to always keep the enemy guessing when you will strike next. He spat a glob of blood from his mouth onto the oriental style rug beneath his feet and wiped the excess with the back of his arm.

"Your girl, huh? I didn't know you were having issues finding a girl without having to purchase her, Everett."

Clicking my teeth, I let out an amused chuckle as I returned to his line of sight.

"How is the little whore, by the way? Last I saw, she was running to the gates at Stone Fortress. I can't imagine a girl like her being very—what's the word —compliant?"

Arno was trying to get under my skin; he was succeeding, but I would never show him that. My demeanor remained calm and stoic as I sat in the chair opposite him.

"Call her a whore again, Arno, and see what a bullet between the eyes feels like." The way Dean spoke was almost demonic. He was bloodthirsty, and I wouldn't put it past him that he would indeed smell blood tonight.

"Oh, what do we have here? It sounds to me that

more than one of you has started developing some type of attraction to the little firecracker. Am I right?

I looked at Dean from the corner of my eye, but his gaze remained locked on Arno, guns still pointing at the twin's temples. The anger that was vibrating off his chest was worrisome. I, too, wanted to kill this fucker, but we all knew we couldn't do that just yet.

"She must have the tastiest pussy this side of London if the reaper over there is defending her." That's all he had to say.

As if he were indeed the reaper, Dean turned his gun to Arno and let off one shot. His bullet landed right below Arno's right shoulder, blood coating the fabric of the chair he was sitting on.

"Motherfucker!" Arno grabbed hold of his shoulder and pulled it away to inspect the blood that coated his hand. I looked to Dean, and his expression was pure evil. Colson on the other hand was smirking, his chest vibrating from holding in his laughter. Just then one of the twins shifted in his seat, causing Colson's attention to snap back to the couch. He held two guns, one in each hand, his smile quickly dissolving as he eyed the twins.

"Try me. Move again and see how easy it is for me to end your life." Mr. Charming, himself, was the master of turning off his charm and turning on the killer who lurked just beneath his handsome demeanor. Sitting in my chair, I spread my legs a little wider, sinking into the plush armchair as I stared daggers at Arno.

He was still wincing at the pain Dean had inflicted, but I was still staring at his now deformed nose, which lay crooked across his face.

"I'm going to ask you this once, Arno. What makes you so bold that you can send your guys to our house, or even send these two fuckers"—I gestured to the twins—"to try and take her from us?" The look he gave me was all confusion.

"What the fuck are you talking about? Why do you think that bitch is so important that I would send any of my guys to your place? Fuck, these two assholes did their little stunt all on their own. Clearly, they learned their lesson, by the looks of it."

I looked to the twins, but neither of them could look me in the face. I gave Colson and Dean a look as if to ask "you think he's telling the truth?" Silence filled the room a long moment as I pondered his answer.

"Why the hell do you think I believe you?" I turned my gaze back to Arno, trying not to laugh at the pain plastered on his face. Yeah, I was fucked up, enjoying his pain.

"Fucking hell, Stefan, tell him already," Arno directed his question to Stefan, who was sitting with his brother on the couch. The look on Stefan's face told me enough. He was scared shitless and knew he had fucked up that night.

"Shit, fine. We saw you guys at the restaurant and thought it would be funny to grab her. Obviously, we failed." He waved his hand in front of his face, which was riddled with black-and-blue bruising.

Dean let out a deep growl of laughter. "You're welcome," he said behind him, still pointing his gun at Stefan's temple.

I rubbed my hand down my face. If this asshole didn't send the three men to our house, who the fuck was it? Who had the nerve to challenge me in my own home? If Arno and his men hadn't tried to break in, there was someone else out there who wanted Sloan. My veins ran hot, as anger boiled in my core. As much as I hated this fucker sitting in front of me, I should have known he didn't have the balls to pull a stunt like that. Pushing up from the armchair, I walked over to where Arno sat and positioned myself in front of him. Looking down at him as he clutched his shoulder in pain, I holstered my gun and placed my hands in my pockets.

"Let this be a warning to keep your guys on a tighter leash next time." I practically spat my words at him, before turning on my heels and nodding to the guys. Both Dean and Colson kept their weapons drawn, before following me to the back door. I heard the familiar crunch of a fist hitting someone's face and knew that was a parting present from Dean. He was probably mad he couldn't kill anyone. So, a fist to the face would suffice.

I didn't turn around as I said, "We should do this again sometime."

CHAPTER 26

SLOAN

After the guys left, I couldn't sit still. My nerves were on edge, thinking about the possibility of one of them getting hurt over me. Pacing in the kitchen, I could sense the guys, Stone and Cain, getting annoyed with my constant movement, so I decided to go swimming. Changing into my suit, I informed them I would be in the pool, but instead of just watching me through the glass door, they both just followed me out. Each propped themselves on a lounge chair and watched me intently. I knew the guys just wanted to keep me safe, but this helicopter behavior from the two meatheads was starting to be a little much.

Rolling my eyes, I tossed my towel to the side and jumped in. The water was warm, bathwater warm. I was thankful because the outside temperature had dropped significantly and the chill in the air gave me instant goosebumps. I decided to swim laps, freestyle being my favorite, in hopes of clearing my mind of the possibility that someone would get hurt tonight.

I quickly got into a rhythm, and my motions became fluid and smooth as the water danced over my body with every stroke and kick I made. This was where I felt most at peace. The water was my second home, my therapy when I needed to escape the chaos in my head. I focused on my breathing with each tilt of my head. Breaking the water's surface, I inhaled the cold, crisp air that made up the night.

I don't know how long I was swimming for, but as my body began to feel heavy and sluggish, I knew I'd had enough. Reaching the edge of the pool, I hoisted myself out of the water and found my towel. Shit! It really was freezing outside, and being wet didn't help matters. I wrapped my towel around me and informed the guys I was going to shower. They didn't respond; they just nodded and followed close behind as we stepped through the sliding doors.

"You guys don't have to follow me to the shower. In fact, I don't think the guys would like that very much," I said this over my shoulder, hoping they would take the hint and stay downstairs.

"Fine. Hurry up, though. We aren't supposed to let you out of our sight," Cain replied, sounding every bit annoyed.

I padded my way across the tile floor, leaving puddles of water trailing behind me. Reaching the hallway upstairs, I hesitated a moment as my curiosity slowly got the best of me. Looking from one to the other of the guys' bedroom doors, I had the strong urge to snoop. I know it's not polite to look through someone else's private space, but I just couldn't help myself.

I grabbed the handle of the closest room and turned the knob, pushing the door open. This room was large, larger than the one I was currently staying in. The walls were a soft gray, and in the center of the room, a large king size bed stood, perfectly made with black sheets and comforter. The room was rather empty, in fact. Besides the bed, the only other furniture was a lounge chair pushed up in the corner and a dresser that was rather small, but its length stretched along the opposite wall of the bed. Everything was gray and black. The carpet was a plush gray. It truly didn't look like anyone's room in particular, but rather a spare room that hadn't been touched. The closet doors were open, and the only clothing that hung was a massive collection of suits, all black or gray.

To be honest this room oozed masculinity, and I could only think this room must be Everett's. He was the kind of man who was put together, always dressed like he was on his way to a meeting or maybe a funeral, and everything about him screamed boss. His hair, body, movements, addictive smell, and the way he looked at me as though I were his next prey had my core burning with desire every time his gaze met mine.

I left his room, shutting the door behind me and

headed for the second door. Pushing the door open, I instantly knew this room was Colson's. His room was not as clean as the first one, but his bed was at least made. Well, kind of. The comforter was pulled up over his pillows, giving the illusion it was made. His walls were a soft gray as well, but he had posters hanging on his wall.

The English soccer team was the largest poster stretching the length of one of his walls. I had never watched soccer, so truthfully, I had no idea who those men were. I smiled as I continued examining his room. It felt like I was standing in a college guy's room, not that I had ever been in one, but everything about it screamed guy's room—the way his clothes were scattered across his bed or draped over his lounge chair, or how the opposite wall held a collection of posters displaying several pin-up girls. Some of the girls were naked, while some were barely clothed. This is what I imagined to be any guy's room. Covering the surface of his dresser was a long row of knives. Some big and others small, but all looking just as intimidating as the next.

With that I shuffled out of his room and crossed the hallway to peek inside the last room. I assumed this would be Dean's room, process of elimination I suppose. I pushed the door open and could barely see inside; it was so dark. Flicking on the light, I had to rub my eyes to adjust to the sudden brightness. When I opened my eyes, I knew without a shadow of a doubt this was Dean's room.

His walls were black, his bed was black, and his chair was black. There were several guns that were hanging from his wall. I counted twelve in total. His bed was a four-poster with a black iron frame that gave me *Fifty Shades of Grey* vibes. It didn't scare me— hell, it only sparked my curiosity more. He was the only one out of the three I hadn't slept with. How could all three of these men be so incredible different, yet here I was attracted to all three? What kind of person did this make me? Dean's room wasn't messy. In fact it was relatively clean, like Everett's, but the whole mood of this room was so … dark.

I knew Dean had a dark past from when he had showed me his burn mark, similar to mine. My past was no wonderland either, so because of that I felt closest to Dean. Our souls were tainted, scarred from a traumatic past that forever casted a dark shadow upon us. It was as though we were cut from the same cloth, yet so different in our experiences.

A saddening pressure was building in my chest, and I ached to know more about what made Dean, Dean. Opening his dresser draw, I picked up one of his T-shirts and brought it to my nose. It smelled of Dean, clean fresh linen with a hint of pine forest. I held the shirt out in front of me. It was a simple black shirt, long with a few small holes cut along the neck- line as well as on the back. I took it with me as I left his room, not really sure why. Shutting the door behind me, I headed for my own room to shower.

CHAPTER 27

SLOAN

After showering, I put on Dean's shirt and a pair of black panties and found myself fast asleep, sprawled out on my bed. I tried staying awake to see the guys when they got home, but the two-hour swim I'd done earlier left me feeling completely drained. I was startled awake by the sound of thunder outside my window. Rising up from my bed, I noticed the clock on my nightstand read two in the morning. I wondered if the guys had come home yet?

I got up from my bed and slowly made my way to the hall. All three of the guys' doors were shut, and I didn't want to risk waking them by opening them. I slowly crept down the hallway and made my way to the kitchen for a drink. I hadn't eaten dinner, and my mouth was drier than the Sahara Desert. I was quiet as I tiptoed down the stairs and made my way across the foyer to the kitchen's entrance.

A dark figure stood at the end of the island, both hands were bracing the countertop as his back faced me. It took a moment for my eyes to adjust to the darkness, but it didn't take long for me to realize it was Dean, alone in the kitchen, sipping from a crystal tumbler that was half full of amber liquid. He was shirtless, wearing nothing but gray sweatpants that hung low from his hips. Fuck, why are sweatpants so sexy on a man?

I leaned against the doorframe and watched as the muscles in his back flexed and relaxed with every lift of his glass.

"Was there a reason you came to the kitchen, or are you just going to stare at my ass all night?" His voice startled me from my trance, and I quickly pushed off the archway. How the fuck had he known it was me?

"I was thirsty and came to get a drink. When did you guys get home?"

Dean then turned to face me, and his eyes instantly saw the shirt I was wearing. His shirt.

"You know it's not ladylike snooping in another man's room." His voice was all sex, as he licked some whiskey off his bottom lip. I made my way over to the fridge, opening the door and pulling out a water bottle.

"I was just curious about the man who shares twin scars with me." Opening the bottle, I took two large gulps. His eyes narrowed on me, as though he was trying to read me. "I wanted to know if your darkness was the same as mine." My voice was low, almost a whisper, but the way his head tilted to the side, I knew he'd heard me.

"My darkness is far beyond anyone else's, doll."

I stared at him, wondering what secrets he held deep inside. What pain and torment had he endured? What darkness created a soul like his?

"I'm not trying to compete with who has the darker past. I'm just curious; that's all."

He swallowed the remains of his drink and placed the glass in the sink. He closed the distance between us in two large strides. He was so close I had to look up to see his face. His scent made its way to my nose and straight to my pussy. He must have just gotten out of the shower, because the fresh scent of soap was invading my nostrils.

"I'm going back to bed." Turning to leave, I was instantly halted by a pair of strong hands wrapped around my waist, and soon my feet left the floor. Dean lifted me so fast and placed me on the island. My ass slapped against the cold granite, making me shiver.

"Why are you so curious about me?" His voice was deep as he spread my legs and stood between them. His hands rested on the counter on either side of me. His eyes were steel-gray, and his face was so close to mine that all I had to do was lean forward an inch for our lips to touch. We were breathing each other's air, the mere presence of him had me clenching my core in hopes of stopping the pleasure building between my legs.

"Well?" He tilted his head slightly to the side, waiting for my response.

"I envy you. You don't let your past affect your soul."

"Baby girl, my past created this dark soul. Every shadow, every scar, every ounce of my being—all perfectly mastered by the demons of hell itself. Stained black for the rest of my life. My past is my future." He paused a moment before continuing. "Never envy the devil; he may just want you as company." Brushing his thumb along my lower jaw, he grabbed the nape of my neck with his other hand, pulling my face to his as our lips collided in a bruising kiss.

CHAPTER 28

DEAN

The first time I kissed Sloan I was instantly addicted to her taste, her lips, her scent. Seeing her in my T-shirt, I couldn't fight my attraction any longer. I needed Sloan as much as a shark needs water to survive. Her lips were like candy to me, and I needed more with every taste I got. She didn't pull away either. She kissed me with just as much force that it was as though our mouths were fighting each other, fighting for control. Her hands grasped the back of my neck, her nails digging in enough to leave marks.

I released Sloan's neck as my hands started exploring her bare thighs. She was only wearing my shirt, and I assumed she was wearing panties. Sliding my hands up her thighs and pushing my shirt up, I squeezed her waist hard enough that she flexed her abs against my touch. Slipping my tongue inside her mouth, I could feel my tongue piercing click against her teeth. A small moan escaped her mouth, and I inhaled her sounds. Fuck! I loved the sounds she made.

Her legs wrapped around my waist, pulling me in so that our bodies were flush against each other. My cock pressed hard against her stomach as her legs squeezed me tighter. I swept my hands higher up her stomach until I reached her breasts and squeezed both hard enough to make her moan again.

"Fuck, Sloan, you keep making those sounds and I'm going to lose it."

She arched her body into my touch as I started kissing down her neck. Sloan was intoxicating, and I needed to know what she tasted like.

I pushed back from her grasp and her legs fell from my waist. The look she gave me was pure sex as she eyed my bare chest.

"Take my shirt off, and lay back, now."

She didn't hesitate; she obeyed my every command.

"Good girl."

She removed my shirt in one swift motion and tossed it aside. As soon as her back was against the island top, I pulled her legs closer to the edge. I needed her on my tongue.

I grabbed the sides of her panties and tore them off her. I hoped she wasn't fond of those panties, because they were history. Spreading her legs and exposing her pretty pink pussy, I dropped my face right to her center, giving her one long lick. She was so wet already, and I couldn't get enough as I sucked and licked all her pleasure.

"Dean," she moaned while her hands gripped the back of my shaved head, holding me firm to her. Using my tongue ring, I licked and swirled around her clit. Her breathing picked up with every suck of my lips.

"Fuck, Dean, I'm almost there!"

At her comment, my lips curled into a smile, and I picked up my pace. Sloan's fingers dug into my neck just as she yelled through her orgasm, her pussy clenching around my tongue as she rode out the waves of her climax. I couldn't wait any longer. I flipped her around so that her stomach was flat on the counter and her legs hung off the edge. I gripped my hard cock, lining it up with her entrance, pushing just the tip inside her.

"Please, Dean, give it to me!" Her voice was my choice of drug, and without any more hesitation, I slammed my cock fully inside her. She arched her back, swinging her long blonde hair down her back as she screamed her approval. I slowly removed my cock, but not without her protest.

"Don't stop!" she pleaded, looking at me over her shoulder.

I leaned against her back so that my mouth was at her ear. "I want you to beg for it," I whispered, causing goosebumps to prickle her back.

"Please, Dean, I want your dick inside me."

A deep chuckle of satisfaction rose from my chest,

and I gave her just that. I slammed my cock into her tight cunt, again and again and again.

"Fuck, you feel so good."

I reached my hand around her front to find her wet pussy once again and started making quick circular motions as I continued to push deeper and deeper inside her. Just as her pussy clenched around my dick, I couldn't hold on any longer, I thrusted deep inside her, giving her my full release while a dark moan escaped my throat. I held on to her hips tight as my dick twitched inside her.

We stayed like that for a moment, her body slumped across the counter as I lay across her back, kissing my way to the side of her neck. Standing up, I slowly pulled my dick from her pussy and pulled up my sweatpants. She turned around to face me. Draped over her shoulders, her long hair was a mess. I cupped her face, pulling her into a kiss so she could taste herself on my lips.

"About damn time," Colson's voice echoed through the kitchen, breaking our kiss. We both turned our heads to see Colson leaning against the wall, a smile splayed across his face.

"That was hot as fuck."

I couldn't help the smile of satisfaction that pulled at my lips.

CHAPTER 29

SLOAN

"All right, how about some ice cream to cool us all off?" Colson asked, giggling like a schoolboy as he made his way over to the freezer to retrieve some vanilla ice cream. He was wearing only his boxer briefs, which were doing nothing to hide his giant erection. No doubt our little show was the reason for that.

I quickly grabbed my shirt, or rather Dean's shirt, and pulled it on—not that Colson hadn't seen me naked already. Picking up my panties, I realized they were unsalvageable and tossed them in the trash.

"Better to just not wear panties anymore." Dean's whisper in my ear had me wet all over again. Fuck, these men were going to be the death of me.

Colson grabbed three bowls from the counter and placed them on the island.

"Better grab another, bro. Couldn't sleep with the

moaning that was echoing throughout the house." Everett's voice was full of sleep as he sauntered his sexy half-naked body in the kitchen. My cheeks pinked at his comment, but I glanced at Dean who gave me a sly wink. Everett was wearing gym shorts and nothing else. Like I said, these guys were trying to kill me.

Colson proceeded to dish a bowl of ice cream for everyone and then slid the bowls across the island to us. Everett leaned back on the opposite counter, picking up his bowl and taking such a large bite that I wondered how he wouldn't get brain freeze.

Dean and I both sat at the barstools beside one another, and Colson stood beside the fridge while each of us enjoyed our dessert. The room was quiet, only the sound of our spoons scraping the bowls echoed in the air. Not being able to take the silence any longer, I asked, "How was your little outing? I'm glad to see you all back in one piece. That's a good start." I looked up at Everett for a response.

Even though Dean had said earlier no one was the boss, but rather they worked together. There was just something about Everett that gave off the leader vibe. He was the one to buy me at Stone Fortress, and the way the other two always stood the slightest bit behind him gave him the appearance of the alpha in this pack. The fact that Dean and Colson were also looking at Everett gave it away as well.

"Well, we didn't kill anyone, love, if that's what

you're asking." Even though he said it as a joke, I had a feeling he was dead serious.

"Yeah, unfortunately," Dean said in between a spoonful of ice cream.

"Aww! Poor Dean, mad he didn't get to add another kill to his body count," Colson said mockingly. A spoon flew across the kitchen, smacking Colson in the side of the head with a loud whack.

"Fuck, bro, that shit hurt!"

I tried to hold in my laughter, but the smear of ice cream that dripped down the side of Colson's face had me biting the inside of my cheek to keep from smiling. I stared into my bowl, swirling the ice cream, which was quickly melting into a pile of cream and sugar. A strong hand grabbed my wrist and pulled the spoon from my grasp in mid swirl.

"Hey, I wasn't done with that!" My tone came out a bit whinier than I had meant for it to be, but the look Dean gave me as he scooped his ice cream with my spoon, placing it between his delicious lips, had my heart beating a little faster.

"Looks like you were done to me," Dean said, licking the spoon clean as his tongue ring clicked against the metal.

I had to look away to keep my libido in check. Just remembering how he used that piercing not ten minutes ago had a fire igniting in my core once more. I needed to change the subject before I found myself sprawled on the counter for round two.

"Did you learn anything about who tried to break

into the house, or why the twins tried to take me? What the fuck is wrong with Arno anyway?" I directed my question to Everett once more. Finishing his ice cream, he placed the bowl in the sink and leaned on the counter, right in front of me.

"Well, there is a lot wrong with that man, but it wasn't him or his men that orchestrated the break-in. The fucking twins tried to win brownie points by kidnapping you—a Capture the Flag type of game, if you want to call it that—but the two incidents aren't connected."

The room fell quiet again. A dark shadow filled the space we occupied. Slowly it became clear to me. The person in charge of trying to kidnap me, apart from the incident with the dumbass twins, was still out there—still plotting his next attempt. My blood ran cold, or maybe it was the ice cream, but I started to become more aware that I was not safe beyond the walls of this house. The tension in the room started to suffocate me as my new reality sunk in. My fear was starting to boil over from my stomach to my chest. My breathing soon became ragged, and my fear was quickly turning into a full-blown panic attack.

"Shit, are you okay?" Colson asked but I couldn't respond. Hell, I felt like I couldn't even breathe.

Everett's hands were on me faster than I could blink, he pulled me from the barstool and sat me on the counter, the cold granite biting my skin. His hands cupped either side of my face. "Breathe, Sloan, you need to breathe." Everett's tone was so soothing, so calm, but the tightening in my chest was only getting worse.

"Fuck, bro, get her some water or something," Colson demanded of Dean as he quickly slid from his barstool and reached for a water bottle from the fridge.

The room was slowly going black as tunnel vision started to cloud my eyesight. I was about to pass out. Just as the sight of Everett's bare chest quickly started to fade in front of me, his lips were on mine.

CHAPTER 30

SLOAN

The tension I was holding in my shoulders fell as Everett's lips brought me from the edge of darkness. His hands still cupped my face, keeping me upright. It was like he was breathing for me, allowing me to stay in the present. His lips were soft against mine, gentle and caressing. I kissed him back as I opened my mouth to his, our tongues massaging against one another. His touch kept me grounded, kept me from slipping into the fear that was quickly consuming me. Suddenly I forgot why I was even panicking at all.

He spread my legs with his abdomen allowing himself to step closer to me. Our lips refused to let go. A moan bubbled from my core, slipping between our mouths.

"Fucking hell," Colson's voice invaded my ears, and I couldn't help the smile that spread across my face.

Everett pulled our lips apart, and I groaned in protest, but when I saw the look on his face, I realized he, too, didn't want this to end. He stared into my eyes, his lips puffy, as he curled his bottom lip exposing his teeth.

"Are you alright, love?" The way he called me love was more than just his little pet-name. He said it with so much lust, so much fire, that I could have ripped his shorts off his body right then and there. Fuck it if Dean and Colson watched. Hell, they both did have a thing for watching, as I was quickly learning.

"Thanks to you." I hoped that sounded as sexy as I was aiming for. With that, he rested his forehead against mine.

"By the way, where the hell are your panties?" A deep, husky growl escaped Dean's chest as he laughed at his comment. My face, no doubt, had turned a shade of pink as the intensity of the guys' stares held me immobile. Everett pulled away from my face, but not before kissing my forehead one more time.

I remained sitting on the counter. Everett took up the barstool in front of me, while Dean and Colson sat on either side of him. Dean handed me a bottle of water. Thanking him, I took it and drank slow sips. Since I had all three of them together, sitting in front of me and giving me their full attention, I had to ask the question that was burning inside me.

"Are we going to discuss our … uhm … relations

with each other? You guys don't seem to be upset with the fact that ... well ... you know." I couldn't even say it out loud. I had fucked all three of them, thanks to tonight with Dean. Had it been my plan? No, but it just happened.

All three of them were so different in so many ways. Everett was, indeed, the boss. He was caring and soothed my soul. Just when I thought I was about to forfeit and allow the darkness to overcome me, he had brought me back to the light. He was the anchor I never knew I needed. He was possessive and controlling in his everyday life, but also in the bedroom. One minute he had a bruising hold on me, the next his touch was as light as air, making me crave him even more.

Colson was my Prince Charming. When we had fucked in the pool, it was perfect. His touch was liquid and glided over my skin in the most intoxicating way. He made me feel like I was floating, his hold on me making me feel safe enough to let go completely. I had surrendered to him in that pool.

Colson was the definition of the world's best cuddler. The way he had held me, swirling me in the water after we played Truth or dare? was what every woman dreamed of in a man—someone to cuddle her, make her feel all warm and fluffy inside. This was Colson.

Now Dean. He's different. Dean was the part of me that I never wanted to let escape, yet he was the only one who could tame the darkness inside. I feared him, and we were the most alike. We'd seen the darkness, we'd fought the darkness, and we'd welcomed the darkness. He was intimidating, he was rough, and he was the shadows of the demons themselves. We had a connection that I didn't have with the others. I looked at him and saw pain, and when he looked at me, I knew he saw the same. I knew there was more to him, and I wanted to be his light in the darkest of days. There was more to Dean, and I intended to find out more about him. Even if that meant I had to expose all of myself to him.

The guys looked back and forth at one another, and I was starting to feel as though they had a telekinetic ability, because the smiles they shared were pure mischief.

"Look, Sloan. If you're asking if we're mad that we've all been with you, the answer is no. We've shared everything with each other since we were boys, but I can't say that we've ever shared a woman." Everett leaned back in his barstool as he spoke, his pec muscles flexing while he crossed his arms. "I feel as though I can say for all three of us, we don't mind sharing our time with you, as long as you're fine with this polyamorous thing we have going on." Everett looked to the left and then the right, both Dean and Colson gave nods of agreeance.

I let out a breath of satisfaction, because in all honesty I didn't want to be the reason these three guys bashed each other's heads in.

"What do you say, gorgeous?" Colson was giving

his most charming smile, showing off his dimples as he curled up his lips at me.

I didn't answer right away. I looked over at Dean first. He was leaning way back in his barstool, his legs spread wide. His sweatpants hugged the delicious *V* at his hips, and his arms were crossed in front of his bare chest. His face was neutral, but as soon as I caught his gaze, he lifted one eyebrow at me, smug as all hell. That was the only answer I needed from him. All three of them were OK with sharing me.

Satisfaction pooled in my belly. At this moment I hadn't realized how quickly I had fallen for these three. I didn't want to choose. In fact, if I couldn't have all three of them, I wouldn't have any at all.

"What would you say if I told you all I didn't want this relationship thing?" I was lying, shit was I lying, but I didn't want to sound desperate. I knew I wanted this. I wanted *all* of this. A deep chuckle drew my attention to Dean.

"I call it bullshit." Dean stood up from his barstool and walked right in front of me, practically pushing Everett aside. He leaned into me so that we were face-to-face, his hands bracing on the countertop on either side of me. "From the sounds of you begging me earlier, I would say you are just as much into this as the three of us."

He was right—I was 100 percent all in. His face was mere inches from mine, his bare chest radiating so much heat. He was an inferno, and I wanted so badly to touch him. I could easily do so. He was so close that I would only have to lift my hand just slightly, and we would be touching.

I was staring at the tattoos covering his chest. They were beautiful, just like him. He grabbed my chin lightly, pulling my gaze to his face. His smokey gray eyes waited patiently for an answer he already knew.

"I'm in," was all I could muster. I could have sworn a smile touched the corner of his mouth, but before I could return the gesture, his lips were on mine in a possessive kiss. I kissed him back, almost a silent gesture of a deal between the two of us. This was our way of sealing the deal. Just then his hand grabbed my bare pussy, cupping me with his callused hand.

"You're mine now." He pulled away from our kiss just slightly to say these words, our lips still touching as he spoke. My breathing increased at this promise, and I knew I was in way over my head with these three.

He pulled away after one final kiss, backing away and giving me a devilish grin. I was pudding in this man's hands, and he damn well knew it. I squeezed my thighs together, feeling the undeniable wetness that now pooled between them.

"Hell yeah!" Colson yelled as he clapped his hands together and stood in front of me. He grabbed my face between his hands and pulled me into his own embrace, kissing me softly—his version of sealing the deal. I chuckled as he pulled away and I met his eyes, giving me a sly wink. Stepping back, he let Everett make his way over to me.

Everett spread my legs slightly and stood between them. He then placed his hands in his shorts pockets and stared at me for a moment—his face stoic and unreadable. He licked his bottom lip as he leaned his head back slightly. Damn, this man was a piece of art.

"You want this, love? Us? This life? Be careful with how you answer, because if you indeed say yes, this is it. You're ours, and there's no going back."

Everett's words gave me chills, as tension vibrated from his chest. I wasn't sure how to take his warning. Did he want this like Dean and Colson? Or did he want me to say no? His body language was giving nothing away while he stood his ground in front of me. Pondering his question, I stared at his chest, watching it rise and fall with each breath he took.

Taking a deep breath, I finally responded, "I've never belonged to anyone before. I've never felt safer in my entire life as I do when I'm with you three. When you say there is no going back, what is there truly to go back to? A life without passion, without people who care about me, a life of being invisible and alone. I never want to go back. If you'll have me, I would like to stay." I looked down at that last comment, not knowing what he would respond with. He didn't take long to respond, his hand gently lifting my face by my chin so that we were face-to-face.

"Whether you said yes or no, you were already ours." Everett kissed me then—a deep, possessive kiss, as his hand found the nape of my neck and held me so tight to his lips that I felt they may bruise. His other hand ran the length of my abdomen, where he lifted the hem of my shirt and exposed my wetness. He cupped my pussy and squeezed me tight enough to hurt.

"This is ours, love. We share between us, but we sure as hell don't play well with others, especially things that belong to us, and only us. Understood?"

He started rubbing his thumb against my clit, and all I could do was shake my head in agreeance. "Good." He pulled away from me before throwing me over his shoulder, exposing my ass to the entirety of the kitchen. "I call dibs tonight." With that he smacked my ass, and I let out a yelp as he started carrying me to the stairs.

"Sleep well, boys," Everett shouted over his shoulder to Dean and Colson, who just watched us leave.

I caught them both smiling as they high-fived each other a victory they'd all won, and I was their prize.

CHAPTER 31

SLOAN

I spent the next couple of weeks becoming very, very familiar with my new roommates. I learned that Colson was the king of cuddles—his touch was gentle and left me feeling like I was his very own princess in a fairytale where we starred as the main characters. Dean was adventurous in the bedroom. He needed to be in control. His touch was rough and bruising, but he was no villain. I did things with him that I had never, ever thought I would do with any man. He brought my inner animal out, as we experimented with ropes, chains, and pain—lots of pain. I never left his room without a new bruise on my fair body, and I loved it.

Everett was a beautiful combination of the other two. He was incredibly in tune with what my body wanted and needed. He knew when I craved his gentle touch, his lazy fingers gliding over my soft skin.

The way he caressed my body brought me over the edge of the most delicious orgasms, but when I needed the more aggressive Everett, the one who loved to choke me just enough, he was happy to oblige. He was my own Dr. Jekyll and Mr. Hyde—my hero and my villain. I had become irrevocably infatuated with these men, and there was no going back.

The days passed with little to no issues from possible kidnappers, murderers, psychopaths, or any other type of person who was currently on the lookout for me. Life with the guys was comfortable. As much of an introvert as I thought I was, waking up with the guys was filling a void in my heart I didn't know I had.

I hadn't slept in my own bed since our agreement in the kitchen that night. I found myself always falling asleep with one of them, and I had never craved touch as much as I did now. I was starting to become attached to them in more ways than just sex. When one of them was gone, doing Shadow things, my anxiety over their safety reached new levels. My chest physically ached until they returned. This feeling of emptiness when one of them was gone was something I had never experienced before. Never had I cared for another person over myself, which was selfish really, but in my own defense, I had never had people in my life worth caring about.

Rubbing my eyes, I sat up, remembering I was in

Dean's room. We all played Mario Kart last night and decided the winner would win me for the night, and if I won, I got to choose. In all reality, I won either way, because a night with any of the guys was a night worth spending. Of course, Dean won, since he was definitely the best at Mario Kart, and Everett and Colson huffed disapprovingly at their loss. Dean slapped my ass, indicating for me to head to his room. I did as I was instructed, smiling to myself at the fun we were going to have.

He tied me to his bedpost and chose a velvet blindfold to place over my eyes. I was left in total darkness. Then Dean's hands made quick work of removing my clothes, but he left on only my thong, which did nothing at hiding the slickness that had developed between my legs as he undressed me.

I never knew what Dean was going to do next; that's what made me crave him even more. His tongue licked and nipped every inch of my body, setting fire to my core. Once his tongue piercing found my clit, I almost came right then. Both Dean and Colson had tongue piercings and were expert at using them. With my hands tied above my head, and my legs spread wide enough to reach the bottom two posts, I was incapable of any movement. Dean had access to every inch of my body, just the way he liked it. His tongue played me like a puppet master, igniting the bundle of nerves and sending me into a euphoria that I could happily stay in the rest of my life. He thrust two fingers inside me as I rode out the waves of the first orgasm, which made me bow my back against his touch.

"You like that, baby doll, don't you?" It wasn't a question, his voice a husky breath. He knew how much I loved his fingers dancing against my walls, making me moan, as he played me like a guitar. While his fingers were deep inside me, bringing me to the edge of a second orgasm, his mouth was kissing my inner thigh with gentle nips and bites as he went. Just then an unfamiliar feeling rose from between my legs.

"Sit still. I'm going to try something new." His fingers were still rubbing my inside walls, but another finger reached lower, pushing on my back hole and causing my toes to curl. His finger continued to push inside me, and the sharp sensation had me yell in pain. "Relax, baby, don't tense or it'll hurt worse."

With the promise of pain, I slowly released the tension just as cold liquid spread across my entrance.

"This will help some. Do you trust me?" His voice was full of lust and sex.

"Yes," I managed to get out, a breathy moan. Spreading the lube across my ass, he reintroduced his finger to my back door. Slowly he pushed inside me, the sharp pain dissipating into a dull ache, and finally when his finger was fully inside, the pain became instant pleasure.

"Atta girl."

He pulled his finger out and pushed back in until I was stretched out enough for him to get two fingers inside me. His pace was slow as he brought me to the top of another climax. He knew it too. Just then he slammed two fingers into my pussy and two fingers into my ass, hard. I fell off the invisible cliff and slammed face first into the wall of pleasure. I screamed my release as my back bowed in an exorcist type of way. Sweat beaded my forehead as he slowly withdrew from both my holes.

The dip of his mattress indicated he had stood up, and I was alone on his comforter, my breathing so ragged that I hardly felt when he knelt back down. A humming noise filled the room, and I smiled as his lips kissed my throat, then my chest, all the way down to my navel.

"Keep still." Before I could ask what he was doing, a vibrating sensation touched my ass, causing me to flinch. "I said stay still."

I obeyed. He pushed the vibrating toy fully inside my ass, and I screamed at the sudden pleasure it was causing me. I felt as though I couldn't catch my breath, the pain mixed with pleasure that the vibration was creating. I couldn't help the continued moans that slipped out of me.

"Fuck, Dean." I needed his dick inside me, now.

"Ask me nicely." Even though I couldn't see him, I knew he was smiling down at me. He loved to hear me beg, and I was about to give it to him.

"Dean, please, I need you now!" I practically screamed it, just as he slammed his velvety smooth cock deep inside my pussy. One thrust was all it took. One thrust and he had me spinning into a third orgasm that inevitably had me seeing stars. He set his rough, powerful pace that had him joining me in his own release. With a deep moan he thrust fully inside me, squeezing my hips so hard that his fingerprints branded me as his property.

CHAPTER 32

SLOAN

Sitting up from his bed, I looked over to see he was still fast asleep. The sheets were just covering his lower hips, as my chest lay bare. His breathing was even and slow. I slipped from the sheets as to not wake him and found a shirt to pull over my bare body. As I reached down to grab my panties, a sore ache flew throughout my body. I was so fucking sore. Every muscle in my body ached, the rawness between my legs had me smiling as I recollected the night's activities.

Quietly, I pulled on my panties and slipped from his room. It was dawn, the light shining in through the windows just barely. I made my way down the hallway to the stairs, tiptoeing, not wanting to wake the other two. Making my way to the kitchen, I flipped on the coffee maker and began grinding my beans. I opened the fridge, retrieving eggs, bacon, and milk for my coffee.

I missed making breakfast. It was my favorite meal of the day, but since one of the guys was always awake before me, I took it upon myself this morning to wake up a bit earlier to make them some food for once. I couldn't complain, though. Most of the time Everett made us breakfast, and I was quick to realize he was the best cook in the house.

Once the beans were grinded, I started the drip, filling my glass mug beneath the smooth velvety stream of coffee that was flowing. I filled the steel container with milk and started to steam the white liquid into a perfect consistency. Once the texture was a puffy warm cloud of goodness, I slowly poured it over the espresso I brewed. And once the foam turned into a dome shape, almost on the verge of overflowing, I stopped and sprinkled a little cinnamon on top.

I missed being a barista; there was something calming and hypnotic about making the perfect cup of coffee. You know when you're alone, but all of a sudden you get the feeling of someone watching you? Like your subconscious is yelling at you to turn around because someone is literally right there?

As soon as I finished sprinkling the cinnamon atop the foam, I had a heavy feeling someone was standing behind me. I set the coffee mug gently down on the counter in front of me. I fisted my hands and spun around as quickly as I could.

"Whoa, sweetheart, you trying to kill me?" Colson

grabbed my wrists and spun me back around so that my back was pressed against his hard, bare chest.

"Shit, Colson, you scared me to death." I let out a deep breath I hadn't noticed I'd been holding. I leaned my head back against his shoulder, smiling up at him. "You're lucky I put my coffee down, or I would have had to kill you for making me drop it."

He laughed a sweet, sleepy laugh as he buried his face into my neck, inhaling my scent.

"I'm sorry, darling, I didn't want to interrupt you. You looked too cute playing barista."

"You know, it's a good thing you're cute," I said, pulling away from him so I could see his handsome face. He really was incredibly handsome, even first thing in the morning. His blond hair was pulled back into his classic man bun that he constantly wore. Several strands framed his face. I couldn't help but tuck a loose strand behind his ear before pulling him in for a kiss.

Colson smelled of citrus and sea salt, as if he'd just gotten back from a morning surf. He definitely had the California surfer guy look, and now he even smelled like one. His skin was a deeper shade than the other two guys, a permanent tan all year round. Lucky bastard.

"How are you so handsome?" I asked, stepping out of his embrace to start making him a coffee to match mine.

"I could ask you the same," he said as he stretched his arms above his head. He didn't have a shirt on, typical. He only wore a pair of black sweats that hugged his hips right at that delicious *V*. Finishing up his coffee, I padded my bare feet over to where he sat at the island and pulled up a barstool beside him.

We both sat in silence, sipping our coffee in utter bliss. This was my favorite part of the day—silence, stillness, and fresh coffee made by yours truly. Colson was not so much a morning person, but I was thankful it was him to join me this morning.

"So, what's on the agenda for the day?" Colson asked between sips of his coffee.

To be honest I wanted to go somewhere, escape the confines of the house for a bit. I knew, however, that was out of the question. Since the guys hadn't figured out who was behind the attacks, we had decided that I would stay at the house until the situation was handled. It had been a few weeks, and I was starting to get cabin fever. I knew Everett wouldn't go for it, and honestly, I couldn't blame him.

"Well, between you and me, I just want to go for a drive somewhere, anywhere really. I'm going stir crazy just being cooped up here all the time."

Colson was looking at the side of my face as I kept my eyes forward. I knew he was going to say no, so I didn't have the courage to look at him. I just waited for the inevitable to come while I continued sipping the remains of my coffee.

"I think we can arrange something." Everett's voice drifted through the air as he stepped through the kitchen threshold, pulling on his white shirt. His hair was wet, and I caught water droplets glistening his abs before his shirt so rudely concealed them. The scent of fresh soap and pine filled the kitchen air and I inhaled deeply.

"Really, are you serious?" I asked, not entirely believing him.

"Yeah, are you serious?" Colson sounded equally as shocked as I was. We both shared a glance as if we were anticipating him to yell "just kidding!"

"There will be rules and precautions, but I need to get out of this house for a bit as well. I feel like the walls are starting to close in on me." Everett looked to me and Colson and then to our now empty coffee mugs. He looked at me with his best can you please make me a coffee, too, face, and I smiled at how boyish he looked. I stood up, narrowing my eyes, and gave him a small smile before heading to the coffee maker. As I walked past him, he pulled me into his embrace, kissing my forehead.

"Thanks, love," he whispered in my ear, his warm breath making me shiver. Everett made his way to the barstool I was sitting at moments ago and plopped down in the midst of a yawn. I started the coffee making process all over again, however, it didn't bother me; it was therapeutic.

"Better make another for me, doll," Dean's husky morning voice echoed down the staircase and throughout the foyer, making me grin. How easy I had become a sucker to these men and their pet names for me. From sweetheart to love to doll, and now darling being the new favorite. I couldn't decide which one I liked most.

Reaching on my tiptoes, I grabbed another mug for Dean, but found myself straining harder than I anticipated, trying to reach another mug.

"Here, let me get it before you knock all the glasses on top of you." Dean was right there behind me, pressing his hard body against my back as his long arms reached right over my hand, while he grabbed the mug I was reaching for. Setting the mug in front of me, he kissed the top of my head and gave my ass a firm grab.

"Ouch, Dean, I'm sore," I hadn't meant to say that so loud, but both Everett and Colson laughed, knowing exactly what we were up to last night. Dean just gave me a cheeky smile before hopping onto a barstool at the counter beside me.

"So, can we really leave the house, Everett, or is that your idea of a cruel joke?" I needed to know. The excitement was bubbling up inside me already just thinking about the escape.

"Ugh ... no, the fuck we aren't. We have no more information about who is after you than we had yesterday or the day before." Dean's voice was stern and nonnegotiable. He was looking right at Everett as the two held a stare down, making the room tense.

"We can't keep her locked up forever, Dean. We need to get out for an hour at least. We'll all go together; she'll never be out of our sight." Everett's tone was firm as he challenged Dean. Colson and I just shared glances every now and then as the tension between the two rose to an uncomfortable level. The room was silent, and I was hardly able to stand it any longer. Stepping in front of Dean, I placed my hands on his thighs.

"It will only be for an hour, like he said, just a drive around for a bit to smell the fresh air and just escape the house. We will be fine. I have the best guard dogs in town." I gave him a mischievous wink. He just held my gaze for a moment and then took a long sip of his coffee. I wasn't quite sure how he did that without burning his entire mouth, but Dean was full of surprises.

"Fine, but I want to go on the record for saying this is not a good idea." He addressed this comment to Everett before tilting the rest of his coffee up, finishing the half cup in one large gulp.

"Yay! I'm so excited! Where should we go?" I was jumping with excitement, hardly able to contain my sudden spike of adrenaline.

"Let's take the motorcycles!" Colson shot up with excitement.

"Wait. You guys have motorcycles?" I'd never ridden on the back of a bike before.

"You'll ride with me," Dean said from behind me, wrapping his huge arm around my waist and pulling me into his chest.

"What? No fair. Why do you get to choose who she rides with?" Colson stood from his barstool, his bare chest catching my eye as I roamed over his chiseled chest.

"Because we all know I'm the best rider." Silence filled the room as if they were considering his statement.

"Fine, she rides with you, but slumber party in my room tonight, sweetheart." Colson shot me his signature wink, and I melted into his eyes.

"Deal," I replied, exchanging a wink back at him.

"Are we settled, gentleman? Have we all got what we wanted out of this?" Everett's eyes drifted from Dean to Colson back to Dean. Both guys just nodded their heads in agreeance.

"Good. Now that that's settled, I'm going to take what I want now." He stood up and walked over toward me. Scooping me up with his arms, he smiled at me before walking me straight upstairs to his room.

CHAPTER 33

SLOAN

"Since those two fuckers get you all day, I want you now, in my room, under my sheets, with me buried so deep inside you, you'll forget those pricks' names." He clicked open his door with his foot and flipped the light on with his shoulder.

"I'd say that is a fair bargain." My cheeks heated with his promise. Tossing me onto his bed, he stood at the end, looking down at me with a hungry look in his eyes.

"Take off that shirt, love, you won't be needing it. Matter of fact, take those panties off while you're at it." Doing as I was told, I sat up and removed my shirt in a way that I hoped was sexy. Pulling my knees to my chest, I grabbed the sides of my panties and slowly pulled them down my thighs. He licked his bottom lip as I sat completely naked on his bed with my arms behind me and knees pulled up just slightly.

"Fuck, you are perfect, love." He knelt on the edge of his bed, his chest bare to me, and only his shorts hugging his hips.

With one hand he grabbed my ankle and yanked me closer to him, causing me to fall on my back. Here was the playful Everett, the predator hunting his prey. His dark eyebrows furrowed as he peered at me through hooded lids. He licked his lips once again while he lowered his head to my abdomen. He started kissing my stomach lightly, causing goosebumps to rise throughout my body. I closed my eyes at his touch and savored every kiss, every lick, every nip he gave me. His head wandered lower, and I subconsciously spread my legs, knowing exactly where he was going next.

He licked me from my ass to my clit in one long, lazy motion, making me shudder beneath him. Stopping at my clit, he swirled his tongue around and around until I was a panting mess.

"Everett, don't stop, please," I begged, my orgasm building within me. He didn't stop, either, but continued—holy fuck did he continue. In moments I was a moaning mess as I climaxed so hard that I thought my heart had skipped a beat with how short of breath I was. He lifted his head from between my thighs, my release coating his face. He licked his lips, as he smiled at the taste of me on his tongue.

"Fucking delicious, love." He leaned in and kissed me hard, placing his hand on my neck as if to pin me down from escaping, but I wasn't going anywhere.

He lay his hard body atop of mine, and I could feel his hard erection pressing into my stomach.

"Lay on your back," I told him, and, to my surprise, he didn't reject my demand. After he rolled onto his back, I grabbed the sides of his pants, pulling them off and freeing his erect cock. I straddled his legs. Placing one hand on his base, I looked right into his crystal-blue eyes as I opened my mouth to him. My tongue slid down his impressive length, savoring his velvety smooth skin while I took him deep in my mouth.

"Fuck, yes. That's a good girl." His words were a breathy moan as his hand threaded through my hair. I continued to suck up and down his cock, taking him in so deep at times that my eyes watered as I gagged. He set a rhythm, fucking my face until I was gasping for air at times. My eyes were a watery mess as his cocked reached the back of my throat and his release shot down my throat while a growl-like moan came from his chest. He released my hair as I swallowed his release and then sat up, still straddling his legs.

He grabbed my hips and yanked me on top of him, kissing me so hard I knew he could taste himself on my mouth. He spun us around so that I was now beneath him, a firm hand grasping my neck. He parted my legs with one of his knees, and I felt his cock teasing my entrance. Pulling away from my face, he asked, "How bad do you want it?"

I lifted my hips toward his already erect cock. This man was a whole new species if he was able to go to round two already. I nudged his cock with my wet pussy in a silent plea. He was still grasping my neck.

"Everett, I need you inside me."

His eyes glossed over me—a man possessed with lust on his mind. He lined up and slammed so hard inside me that I slid up the mattress a bit.

"Fuck!" I yelled out. A deep laugh reverberated in his chest. He leaned down so his face was beside mine and his mouth was at my ear.

"I can hardly handle hearing you moan their names some nights, love. Some nights I want to say fuck it with this deal, kick down their doors, and punish you for saying another man's name on your pretty lips."

I knew Everett was the one with the most reservations about this unnatural relationship we'd created among the four of us. His natural dominance told me this. Then again, he had agreed as much as the rest of us, and at this moment I was already in so deep that there was no way I was going to choose.

"Punish me now then." It slipped from my mouth, and I knew I was going to be sore after this. He quickened his pace as an evil grin stretched across his face. Oh yeah. That was a mistake for me to say, for sure.

His thrusts were so deep and so forceful that if he wasn't holding my neck, I would have slid all the way to the top of the headboard with each thrust of his cock. Even though each thrust brought a sharp sting of pain, it also came with a deep ache of pleasure that was like an electrical current flowing between us.

"I'm so close, Everett, so … " Before I could even finish my sentence, my whole body lit up like a Fourth of July firework. My orgasm was so strong that my skin felt like it was on fire.

Everett came right after me, as if he'd been waiting for me to climax so he could finally let go. He climaxed deep inside of me, and his warm release filled me. He collapsed beside me, our breathing so ragged and out of sync that it sounded like we'd both run a marathon. We lay like that for a long while, his release sliding down my leg was my indication I was in dire need of a good shower. I gave him one more kiss and slid from his bed, making my way to his shower.

"Feel free to join me, if you're feeling up for it." I was feeling playful today, saying this over my shoulder, his eyes menacing as he stood up and followed me into the bathroom. Fuck. Was my body capable of another round? Well, we would see.

CHAPTER 34

SLOAN

Everett and I took our time in the shower. It wasn't until we heard a banging at his bedroom door and heard Colson, who was growing impatient with our little play time and urging us to hurry the fuck up, that we finished cleaning up. Everett had washed my hair and body in the most delicate, delicious way, which had me never wanting to leave his obnoxiously large shower.

Getting out, I wrapped a towel around my wet body and made my way to my own room to find some clothes. I decided on black skinny jeans, black boots, and a black, long sleeve shirt. I decided to blow dry my hair, not wanting to step outside in the cold air with damp hair. I made my way down the hall to the foyer, and what greeted me at the bottom of the stairs was a sight to behold. The guys hadn't noticed me standing at the top of the stairs just yet, so I decided to take a few seconds to appreciate how insanely lucky I was.

The three of them were all wearing dark jeans and long sleeve, black shirts, as I was. Great minds think alike, I suppose. Colson was sitting at the bottom step with his hair pulled back in a tighter, neater bun than I had seen on him before. He was leaning back with his elbows against the stairs, his legs sprawled out in front of him. Dean was leaning against the stair post with his hands in his pockets. Every now and then he would brush a hand over the top of his shaved head. He had a tattoo of a black crow, with shadows laced throughout the feathers, covering the back of his neck. I had never really noticed the detail of the wings until now. It was a masterpiece and one of the best tattoos I had seen. Everett saw me first—his body leaning against the front door as it held him up, hands in his jean pockets, and one foot planted on the door. His black clothing made his eyes brighter than ever.

"Enjoying the view, darling?" Everett made my presence known to the other two, and the fact that I was being a perv by staring at the three of them.

"Fuck, I wish I were inside those jeans right now." Colson was looking at me upside down as he tilted his head backward.

I chuckled at his comment, but more so at the way he was leaning upside down to look at me. I looked to Dean, who was looking at me through narrowed eyes.

"This isn't a good idea, Everett. What if someone

sees her out?" Dean was looking right at me when he spoke to Everett, concern written all over his face.

"It's only an hour, bro. She needs this time." Everett kept his gaze on me, but something about his eyes made me think he agreed with Dean.

"Come, love. We have something for you." Everett tilted his head to the office, and I grabbed the handrail, making my way down the stairs. Colson had already started following Everett into the office, bouncing on his heels with each step as though he could hardly contain his excitement. Dean waited until I reached the bottom of the steps, snaking his hand around to my lower back and pulling me into his side. Leaning into my neck, he inhaled my scent deeply.

"You look stunning, baby doll." His voice was a husky whisper. I shivered at the feel of his warm breath against the sensitive part of my skin, just below my ear.

"I'm only wearing black, Dean." I chuckled, closing my eyes and leaning into his touch. He inhaled me again.

"It's my favorite color." He kissed my neck, and I could have canceled this whole outing right then and there just so he could continue kissing my skin for the rest of the day. Since when had I become this fucking horny, twenty-four seven? Oh yeah, since I now lived with the three hottest men who walked this planet.

Dean's hand ushered me to the office, where Everett and Colson huddled around the desk, hiding something from my view. Stepping across the threshold of the office door, I felt Dean's hand disappear from my back and watched as he joined the other two by the desk.

"What is this like an intervention or something? Yet I don't know what you'd be intervening with besides my coffee addiction, I suppose." I crossed my arms over my chest, which hoisted the girls up a little higher than my push-up bra was already doing. The three of them just smiled at me before they stepped aside from the desk, revealing what they had been hiding.

Lying across the desk was a leather jacket that looked to be my size and on top of it was a gold chain necklace with a small charm of the letter *S* encrusted with small diamonds. My eyes grew twice their size as I approached the desk and reached for the necklace. I gently traced the letter with my finger, a small gasp escaping my lips as I asked, "Is this for me?"

Never in my life had I received anything so beautiful, so elegant, so expensive. I didn't know what to say. The guys didn't reply. Colson lifted the necklace and draped it around my neck, fastening the clasp and pulling my long blonde hair through the chain. Looking down at the charm that now lay flat against my chest, I felt the sting of tears filling my eyes.

"What's wrong, don't you like it?" Colson sounded genuinely concerned that I didn't like their incredible gift.

"Yes, yes, of course I love it, it's just … " I trailed

off, wiping a single tear that now ran down my cheek. "It's just, I have never been gifted anything before."

Silence filled the room once again.

"Well, get used to it, sweetheart, this is only the beginning." Colson pulled me into a tight embrace as his large arms wrapped around my neck, pulling my head to rest against his chest. I fit perfectly in Colson's chest, his arms swallowing me whole and his large frame covering my body. I stayed like that for a moment longer, not wanting to show the guys how emotional this gift had just made me. Colson kissed the top of my head before pulling me from his grasp.

"Here, try this on." Dean held out the leather jacket, unzipping the front for me.

The leather was soft and smelled so new that I couldn't help the sudden inhale I took as Dean pulled the front together and zipped me in.

"Perfection." Dean's eyes met mine, and he stood from his leaning position and towered over me. He cupped my chin with his hand, pulling my face up toward his. He leaned in and kissed me softly, his scent filling my nose.

"Thank you," I managed to say without my voice cracking. Dean dropped his hand, and I looked from one to the other. "Thank you, all of you. This is more than I deserve." My lips curled into a pitiful smile, but it was Everett who spoke next.

"You're wrong. You deserve more, Sloan. You deserve so, so much more." He closed the gap between us, grabbing my hips and hoisting me off the ground as if I weighed nothing to him. He gently sat me down on the desk, parted my legs, and stood between them so that our chests were inches apart.

"You deserve to be treated like the goddamn queen you are. We don't deserve you. You've accepted us when we were the fuckers who stole the world you created for yourself." He grabbed my face between his rough callused hands before continuing. "I can never give you back what we took from you, but I will fight to the ends of the fucking world to ensure no one else ever hurts you again, love."

The guilt they all carried for kidnapping me and bringing me to Stone Fortress weighed on them like a massive lead weight, crushing their chests and suffocating them until they could make things right. What they didn't know, though, was if things hadn't played out the way they had, I wouldn't be here right now.

"I don't want my old life back. If you didn't take that job, I wouldn't be here right now. I believe everything happened for a reason. It happened so I would end up right here with you three in this house, feeling more alive than I have ever felt. This is exactly where I need to be." Instead of a verbal response, Everett kissed me, and he kissed me hard. Electricity flowed from his lips to mine in a possessive kiss that had me feeling weak. A cough behind us had me smiling through our kiss, knowing the guys were getting impatient with our quick make-out scene.

"Fuck, guys, be patient I'm having a moment with my girl."

"Correction, bro, *our* girl. You need to learn to share better." Colson's tone was joking as he grabbed a matching black leather jacket, pushing his arms though the sleeves.

I caught a glance of Dean, who already had his jacket on and was leaning against the doorframe with his hands in his pockets, looking all types of annoyed. I shot him a wink, and I caught the corners of his lips curl into the faintest of smiles. I hopped off the desk and ran my hands down my new sexy as hell leather jacket, admiring the feel and silkiness of the leather.

I clapped my hands together before saying, "All right, who's ready to go!" I was so excited, but, honestly, I had never ridden a motorcycle before, and to say I wasn't nervous would be a lie.

"One more thing. Here, take this, and if anything goes bad, use it." Dean handed me a small black pistol, dropping it in my palm. It was small enough to fit in my hand, but I had never touched a gun before, and the sweat that beaded my forehead was a dead giveaway.

"All you have to do is point and shoot; just don't shoot one of us, love," Everett said from behind me, his chest brushing my back as he stepped closer. I admired the gun—the cold metallic feel against my palm, the weight, which was shockingly lighter than I anticipated.

"I know it's dangerous out there, but do I really need this? After all, I've got the three of you." I looked up to meet Dean's gaze. His face was hard and dark as he looked down at me.

"I only just found you, and I will make damn sure those fuckers breathe their last breath if they even look at you the wrong way. You belong to us, love, and we don't share with others, remember." His eyes were dark, full of fury and violence as if anticipating something dark was coming. This was my living, breathing shadow, and he would undoubtedly kill his way through anyone who placed a hand on me. I believed it, too, just from the simple way he was looking at me. I knew this man would stand in front of a bullet for me. With that, I placed the gun in my waistband and stood on my tiptoes, kissing him gently.

"We will be fine. Now let's go before you guys suddenly change your minds."

CHAPTER 35

COLSON

As much as I needed this ride—we all needed this ride—something heavy was weighing on my chest. I had a pit of darkness in my stomach, making me fear something was coming. Something dangerous lingered in the back of my mind: Things had been too quiet lately, and it was only a matter of time before we could expect another attack. Standing in the office and watching Sloan's excitement at the ride ahead, I couldn't back out now. She had been locked in this house for far too long. She'd obeyed every rule placed on her to ensure her safety, and most of all she had never complained once.

She'd understood the danger she was in and had never tried to sneak out, had never tried to run, and she'd made the most out of her situation. Sloan swam, a lot. She was a natural in the water, and I loved watching her come to life in the pool every single day.

But at this moment she needed more. She needed fresh air on her face, the feeling of speed and freedom, even if it was only for an hour.

We made our way to the garage where the three Harley Davidson motorcycles sat side by side. All three as black as our souls. Everett's was all black, but the shiny black you see on most bikes. Deans was a matte black with matte emblems. He said the gray represented his own shadows, his own demons. Mine on the other hand was shiny black like Everett's, but I had a thing for chrome, so throughout the engine and pipes, chrome sparkled, as the lights illuminated the garage.

"Holy shit! How did I not know you guys had these hiding in here?" Sloan's voice echoed throughout the garage, excitement filling the air. She rushed over to the bikes, gently swiping her hand across the seats.

"Hasn't really been any reason to come in here, has there?" Pulling out my bun, I fastened it into a lower bun, allowing room for my helmet to fit more comfortably.

"True," Sloan replied, shaking her head in agreeance. Dean made his way over to the side wall, where he grabbed an extra helmet for Sloan. He grabbed the full-face helmet for her, no doubt wanting to protect her from the cold. It was not the warmest of days, and now that it was late evening, the sun was quickly fading and taking away most of the day's warmth. Plus, it was fall, almost winter at this point, and the wind would make the ride even colder.

"Here, love, put these on too." Everett handed her a pair of black leather gloves to match her jacket, and she took them willingly.

"How the hell do you fasten this thing?" She was trying to buckle her helmet but had already placed her gloves on, making the simple task now more challenging.

"Here, let me help," I offered, tilting her head up so I could see her straps as I threaded them through the buckle. "There, now you're ready." I sat, patting the top of the helmet and making her head bobble like one of those head decorations people place on the dashboard of their cars. She gave me a double thumbs-up, and I just chuckled at her gesture.

The three of us mounted our bikes, and as soon as Dean was done situating himself, he grabbed Sloan's arm and helped her swing her leg around his bike. That lucky bastard. What I wouldn't do for her to be on the back of my bike, holding tight to my waist. Soon I told myself. As soon as all this shit was over with. I made a mental note to start working harder at finding the fucker who wanted to kidnap her.

Everett clicked his garage door key, making the door open, and he was the first to back out. Following Dean, I was last to leave, clicking my own button to close the garage as we sped down the driveway together.

CHAPTER 36

SLOAN

I wrapped my arms tight around Dean, my hands not being able to touch one another due to his broad form. I rested my hands on his lower abdomen looping my thumbs in his waistband, causing a low rumble to vibrate in his chest.

"Careful, doll. Any lower and I won't be able to concentrate."

I was barely able to hear him over the rev of his engine, but I smiled at the fact I could impact this man so much, just from a simple hand gesture. I snuggled deeper into his back, just as his left hand reached behind him, giving my thigh a tight squeeze. Damn that was hot.

The iron gates at the end of the drive opened slowly, but as soon as they fully opened, we were off like a bat out of hell. Like a couple of wild horses escaping the confines of a corral. The air was crisp and harsh against my legs, but the leather jacket protected me from even the slightest bit of cold seeping in. We were going so insanely fast. I closed my eyes hard as fear started to take hold.

"Relax, I got you," Dean spoke loudly enough so that I could hear him over the howling wind and roar of the engine.

With that small comment, I opened my eyes and turned my head to see in front of us. Empty road. We were all alone. The four of us drifted down the forest-covered back road, swaying between one another. Looking at Colson, he shot me a hand gesture that vaguely resembled the hand gesture surfers do when they say, "hang loose." I smiled under my helmet.

I smiled so big that my cheeks started to hurt. Everett was leading us in front, setting the speed, and we all stayed close. That was one of the rules he set for us—we all stayed close no matter what, and if anything were to go wrong, I was to run and not think twice. I didn't like that rule; it didn't sit well with me. I was not about to leave my guys, even if I did promise. I was not going to let them risk their lives for me.

Pushing that thought aside, since we were only going to be out here for an hour, I looked to the sky. It was full of twinkling stars painted across the clear sky. I started laughing—at what, I was not sure. I just had the intense urge to laugh.

I laughed, letting my voice fill the air around me, fill my ears, and echo throughout my mind. I felt

Dean's back vibrate, and I could have sworn he was laughing too.

Perfection. This moment was the most pure and free I had ever felt in my short life. I was soaring through the breeze, my lungs fully expanding as I filled them with air. Nothing and no one could ever take this moment from me.

We started approaching a town, the streetlights illuminating the dark pavement below us. The town was quaint, small, and exceptionally charming. Small shops lined the main street—a café, bagel shop, boutique, and general store were the first stores I noticed. The town was relatively small. We reached its end in a matter of minutes. I adjusted my grip on Dean's waist just as we picked up speed once more. Leaving the town's lights, the road ahead turned dark once again, the only lights were the ones from the bikes.

I noticed Everett waving ahead of us, and Dean pulled up beside him. We stopped in the middle of the road. The eerie absence of other vehicles made this possible without causing an accident. Dean and I pulled up to Everett's left side, and Colson took up the spot to his right.

"Time to head back." It was a nonnegotiable statement. Everett revved his bike, peeling out first and swinging his bike around, Colson following tight behind him. Dean revved his engine a few times, spinning his tires, whipping us around in an impressively sexy way that had my thighs clenching hard around his lower half.

We watched as the other two sped off ahead of us, just as an ear-piercing shot rang throughout my helmet. Dean's body was pushed back into mine as his body fell limp, his arms falling to his side. We were on the ground, the bike pinning us to the wet pavement. The exhaust pipe quickly burned though my jeans and began melting away layers of skin as my screams echoed in my helmet. I kicked, yanked, and finally was able to free my leg, but not before the pipe left a blistering bloody burn across my calf.

Dean wasn't moving, his huge frame pinned to the road. No amount of my shaking was waking him. Placing my hands over his chest where the bullet ripped through his shirt, I noticed there was no sign of blood. Not a drop. Taking a closer look, I could see what looked to be a vest underneath clothes. Pushing lightly on his chest, I could tell he was wearing a bullet proof vest. He can't be dead. He's just unconscious from the impact. I prayed.

"Dean! Dean, please wake up, please! I was screaming as I yanked my helmet, throwing it beside me. I grasped his face in my hands as I continued screaming for him to wake up, tears falling freely from my eyes clouding my vision.

Everett and Colson still hadn't turned around, their bikes a mere dot in the distance ahead of us, quickly disappearing as they continued.

"Help! Please, someone help!" I screamed,

knowing no one was around us, then it hit me like a knife. A sharp sting stabbed my neck, as a pained scream slipped through my lips. I grabbed my neck to determine the cause of pain—a now empty syringe was hanging from my neck. I yanked it free, just as black spots began speckling my vision. The pavement spun, and the lifeless form that was Dean slowly began swirling in front of me. Fuck, I had been drugged.

"What the fuck? What do you want?" I asked whoever did this. I couldn't see anyone else besides Dean then a voice cracked through the air, just as I faded into darkness.

"Evening, firecracker."

CHAPTER 37

EVERETT

Riding ahead of the others, I started to lose myself in the feel of the wind pushing against my chest, the chill reaching across my exposed face, the smell of the forest drifting all around me. I could hear the rumble of Colson's bike tight behind me, but turned to look behind me to check on Dean and Sloan. Gone. They were gone, his bike not even visible from where we were. I slammed on my breaks so hard that I feared Colson would not be able to stop in time. He skidded to a halt beside me.

"Fuck, where are they?" I screamed as I revved my engine, spinning my bike back around, heading to where we just came. Colson mimicked my movements. Just as I sped away, I heard Colson scream.

"Fuck!"

We both pushed the bikes to their limits, speeding

as fast as we could go. Just as a faint object started appearing in the distance, I throttled my bike to its max. A few hundred yards away, I noticed the object was Dean's bike. His bike lay on its side in the middle of the road, Dean and Sloan nowhere in sight. We both slammed on our breaks, locking up our tires, causing the bikes to skid to a stop. Pushing the kickstand down and jumping off the bike, I knelt down beside Dean's bike, expecting it to tell me anything of what had happened. I noticed a black patch of fabric stuck to the exhaust, and my stomach started to set fire. Sloan had been hurt. The fabric attached to the exhaust pipe told me her leg was pinned long enough for the pipe to have burned through her jeans.

"What the fuck?" I shouted, pacing back and forth on the pavement, leaving Colson kneeling beside the bike.

I pulled out my cell and clicked a number, the dial tone ringing in my ear. The phone only rang twice before a voice echoed through the mobile.

"Everything okay, boss?" Drew's voice was full of concern. I would only be calling him this late if there was a problem, and this was a big fucking problem.

"I need you to run the location on Sloan's necklace. She's been taken and so has Dean."

Colson looked up at me with this new information. I hadn't told the guys I'd put a tracking device in Sloan's necklace, but I needed to make sure we had tabs on her at all times. Now I was fucking happy I had.

"On it. Give me five minutes and I will call you back."

I ended the call, gripping my phone hard enough that I thought it may shatter in my grasp.

"You put a tracker on her necklace?" Colson asked me, standing beside the bike.

"Yeah, I did. Got a problem with that?" I hadn't meant to sound like an asshole, but this was all my fault, allowing this to happen. Now she was gone, along with one of my brothers.

"I'd say that was the smartest move you could have made." Colson's voice was calm and even as he placed his hands in his pockets. My phone rang, and I clicked the answer key almost immediately.

"It looks like they are on the move, traveling southbound at speeds of around sixty-five miles per hour. Wait. Hold up. They are stopping. They just stopped at what looks to be an abandoned warehouse on the outskirts of Newham. I'm sending you the GPS address now," Drew spoke so quickly as he clicked through his computer.

"Get the others. Meet us there now." My voice was dripping with murderous intentions.

"On it." Drew ended the call.

"Let's go; they're in Newham." I looked at Colson, who had already moved Dean's bike off the road and mounted his own, waiting for my instructions.

"Fucking Newham." Colson's words sounded like venom on his tongue.

"Yeah, fucking Newham."

Swinging my leg over my bike, we headed down the road as fast as our bikes could travel. Whoever just took my family was about to pay in the most painful fucking way.

CHAPTER 38

SLOAN

I knew his voice—the deep husky tone, the stupid pet name he'd called me. The image of his face danced in my brain as I fell to the pavement, my eyes closing while the darkness grabbed me and pulled me under. When I woke up, I couldn't see anything yet, my vision still blotchy as I tried to blink about the blackness. The smell of iron and stagnant old water filled my nose. My skin was ice-cold, water soaking all the way to my bones. Dean. Where the fuck was Dean? I sat up with a jolt, still rubbing my eyes to try and wipe my vision clean.

Blinking several times, I was finally able to see the faint glow of a light sitting in the corner of the room, barely illuminating the space I sat in. My jacket was off, my long sleeves ripped up and now looking more like a T-shirt. Standing up, I felt the familiar pain of scorched skin burning my calf. Looking down, I saw the big hole in my jeans where a bright red blister and dried blood now covered the exposed skin. I clenched my teeth so hard at the pain that I was afraid I may break my teeth.

I took a few calming breaths and took in my surroundings, or lack thereof. The room was small, so small it resembled a closet more than a room. There were no windows, no furniture—just a tall lamppost in the corner.

Grabbing the door handle, I expected it to be locked, but to my surprise it wasn't. I slowed my movements, turning the handle slower as to not make too much noise. I needed to find Dean. Was he even here, or did they kill him and leave him on the road for Everett and Colson to find? Fuck, where am I?

I poked my head out of the closet and looked to my right, a long empty hallway. Looking to my left, the same. The ceiling was roughly fourteen feet tall with industrial-sized lamps hanging from exposed beams. I was definitely in an abandoned building or warehouse of some sorts. Water pooled beneath my feet and throughout the hallway, and the only sound I heard was a faint dripping of more water, which soon connected with a puddle beneath. I didn't know which way to go. This place could be huge, and I didn't have time for a tour.

I placed a hand to my forehead and pushed just slightly. The headache that was crushing my brain was starting to rage war against my skull. Just then I reached for my waistband in hopes they hadn't found the gun the guys had given me. Wishful thinking because it was indeed gone. Shit.

I mentally cursed myself and then decided to go in search of Dean. I walked slowly trying not to make too much noise, stepping between the puddles of water. Just then a scream echoed so loud down the opposite end of the hallway, I started jogging toward it. It was a deep manly scream, a painful sound that had me in a full-out sprint in hopes that it wasn't Dean. Please don't be Dean.

I reached a door at the end of the hallway. Grabbing the handle, I found it was locked. Then I reached for a twin door beside it, and thankfully it was unlocked. I swung the door open and my fear took shape in the human form of Van.

He was leaning over Dean, who was chained to a metal chair. He wasn't wearing a shirt. Several cigar burns freshly decorated his perfect chest. My heart cracked at the sight of him.

Blood dripped from an exposed wound on his forehead, right below his hairline. His bottom lip was busted in two places and would inevitably scar. His chest now housed nine fresh cigar burns. The warehouse was completely empty other than Dean, Van, and me.

Dean's head was draped down, the rise and fall of his chest was so rapid as he fought to stay conscious. My eyes burned as tears filled them. I ran to him, grabbing his face in my hands and lifting his head to look at me.

"Dean, I'm here. Stay with me, Dean." My voice was cracking with every word. He didn't respond. His eyes looked as though he barely recognized me. A film of gray glossed over his eyes, and his eyelids were barely able to stay open. I examined his chest, so many burns, so many new fresh burns littered throughout his chest. I bit my bottom lip. A rage I had never felt before boiled in my core. I spun around. Van was smiling wickedly down at me while he continued to puff his cigar.

"You fucking piece of shit!" I yelled at him as my fist connected with his lower jaw. *Damn it! That hurt more than I thought it would.* Van's face jerked to the side, causing his cigar to skid across the wet floor. He grabbed my neck so fast that I didn't see it coming.

"You little bitch! That was a Cuban!" His voice echoed in the warehouse. I grabbed his wrist with my hands in hopes he would relieve some pressure soon, so I could breathe. Choking for air, he finally let me go, and I crashed to the wet concrete floor that covered the warehouse. Coughing and choking until I was able to breathe normally again, I looked up at him. Van was wearing an all-black suit. His pants were baggy, not tailored like most guys' pants, and his jacket was unbuttoned, revealing a black button-down shirt beneath it. His hands were now in his pockets as he stared down at me. Slowly he knelt down by my side, resting his forearms on his legs.

"I bet you never saw this coming, did you, my little firecracker?" His voice was a low whisper, giving me chills, especially when he called me fire-cracker. He brushed a strand of my hair behind my ear and grabbed my chin hard, pulling me to face him. "What? Not feeling confident anymore? Where's the sparkling personality or your witty comebacks?" His hand squeezed my chin even harder. I yanked my face from his and stood to my feet.

"Were you finally over being the bitch boy of the house, and decided to play gangster for the day?"

He shot daggers at me as the scowl on his face squished his facial features. Out of my side vision, I caught a glance of Dean. His face was fully slumped over, but he was still breathing.

"Ugh … don't mind him. He's just getting over a little sedative I had to give him to calm him down a bit." He pushed the side of Dean's head, causing his head to slump to the opposite side.

"Don't you dare fucking touch him!" My words echoed loudly, bouncing off the walls and traveling to the opposite end of the warehouse. He raised an eyebrow at my sudden outburst, and a cruel smile danced across his face. He snapped his fingers, and just like magic two men brought over an additional chair. One of them had rope wrapped around his arm.

"I see you've grown quite fond of these boys over the last couple of months. I can't say that I blame you, with their riches, their mansion, and their endless supply of money. That's every girl's dream, isn't it? I see why you stay. No need to work as … what was it? A barista? No need to scrap by, living hostel to hostel.

Hell, I bet they have servants waiting on your every beckon call."

Two pairs of strong hands grabbed me by the shoulders and forcefully sat me in the chair that was now opposite Dean. I tried fighting them, but as soon as the rope was secured across my wrists and legs, there was no use. I stared at Dean. His broad shoulders hung so low, as blood continued to drip from his wounds. My chest tightened at his drugged state. If he were awake, Van wouldn't stand a chance, I was sure of that. Just then a cell phone rang, and Van pulled out his mobile, clicking the accept button.

"Please excuse me. I must take this. Just make yourself at home." I rolled my eyes at his attempt at humor. I watched Van's back as he stepped away from us, the two other goons following him. When he was far enough away, I turned back to Dean. I needed to wake him up, and fast.

"Dean, Dean, please, baby, please look at me. Wake up. Just open your eyes, please," I begged him in a low whisper. I was unable to hide the tears that were now flowing from my eyes down my cheeks. Nothing. He wasn't moving or saying anything. I tried something different.

"Dean, I never told you this, but the first time we kissed, I dreamt about you that night. I dreamt you snuck into my room that night and took me on my bed. You were rough, dominating, possessive in the most delicious way. I loved it. I never wanted to wake up from that dream. When I did, I tried going back to bed in hopes I would return to the very spot we left off." My chest felt as though it were splitting while I told him of my dream. I couldn't lose him, not like this.

"I knew you had the hots for me."

CHAPTER 39

SLOAN

Dean's voice was so low that I thought I was hallucinating. His head rose just enough that I could see his steel-gray eyes through his hooded lids. The breath that escaped me sounded more like a sob.

"Dean, you're okay," I whispered, a small smile lifting the sides of my lips. He still looked really bad. He'd lost a lot of blood, and his skin was starting to look pale.

"Are you hurt?"

"You're the one bleeding and you're asking me if I'm okay?" I gave him a stern look as if to say I'm more concerned about you.

"Well, are you going to answer me, baby girl?" This man was impossible.

I let out a sigh. "Yes, Jesus Christ, I'm fine."

He smiled at my sudden irritation toward him, but it was Van who interrupted us.

"Awe lover boy is awake; now we can play a bit." Van's gaze fell on me, and if the shiver that ran down my spine was any indication at the danger that was coming, I knew I was in deep shit.

He made his way over to me, standing at my side. He then traced a finger over my hand and up my forearm, giving me chills that caused goosebumps to rise over my skin.

"Don't fucking touch her." Dean's voice was a tone I had never heard before. It was deep, growling, and full of death as he stared right through Van's soul. Van just laughed his loud obnoxious laugh, which made his entire body shake.

"Or what, Dean? I see you're not in the position to be making threats, being chained to a chair and all." Van didn't even look to Dean as he spoke. He just continued to trace his fingers up my bicep and across my collarbone until he noticed something that made him stop.

"Well, well, firecracker, what do we have here?" He knew exactly what it was, the same scar that now peppered across Dean's chest. "It seems you and Dean over here have a thing for cigar burns." Van's glance at Dean had my stomach turning.

"Van, I will rip your fucking head off with my hands. Don't you fucking touch her." His warning scared even me, but Van had found a new sense of confidence since the last time I saw him.

He chuckled at Dean's threat as he pulled a new, fresh cigar from the inside of his coat pocket. My back stiffened, and memories of my father flashed before my vision. I swallowed hard, shaking my vision from my eyes.

I watched Van pull a cigar cutter from another pocket and firmly cut through the end of the cigar. He fetched a lighter next, ignited the cigar and pulled in a few inhales to set the end. Puffs of smoke filled the space around him. I looked over at Dean, tears filling his eyes. It's coming; the pain is coming. His face locked on mine, anger flowing like waves off his bloodied body. He started fighting against his chains, the sounds of iron clanking together filled the open room. The ringing grew louder as Van removed his cigar from his lips, a smile plastered across his face.

"Don't fucking do it, Van!" Dean's voice was louder than the chains holding him down. I closed my eyes, anticipating the pain he would soon inflict.

"Open your eyes, Sloan, look at me!" Dean's voice was a desperate plea.

I obeyed. I opened my eyes, locking on his steel-gray irises that suddenly changed to black. A shadow glossed over his eyes, a fiery darkness that was on the verge of exploding. It was on me. The familiar scent of charred skin filled my nostrils. The feeling of volcanic fire melted each layer of skin, one by one. I screamed in agony, closing my eyes and bowing my back as the cigar set fire to my forearm in a circular pattern. I couldn't hear Dean anymore, the sounds of my scream piercing my eardrum and drowning out any other noises around me.

Van peeled the melted end of his cigar from my skin, revealing a dime-sized hole in my arm, blackened on the edges and deeper than my old scar. It was far, far too deep. I stopped screaming, catching my breath, and blinking away the tears that now flowed freely from my eyes. Just as the pain started to become bearable, I let out a long breath, but a second touch of his cigar had me spiraling on the edge of pain once again. Screams consumed my throat, but this time I was joined by Dean, who was screaming his anger equally as loud.

We sang out our pain in the form of screams, demonic howls that vibrated throughout the warehouse. Anyone within a mile radius would no doubt be able to hear us. I prayed.

CHAPTER 40

DEAN

I had to get out of these chains. The sounds of her screams were chiseling away at my heart, bit by bit, and I couldn't stop the continuous pain Van was inflicting upon her. The image of her face in pure agony as she screamed through each new burn that marked her perfect body had me seeing red, and then black. I was getting out of here. I was going to fillet this man so fucking slowly that he would feel every inch of my knife as I slowly carved away at this pathetic excuse for a human.

I thrashed back and forth, her screams becoming a constant gasp for air. I screamed my frustration while Van lifted his cigar and placed a fourth burn mark, this one on her shoulder where her shirt had slipped down.

"Dean, please!"

She was begging me to help her. Her sobs were

soon cut off by a thick piece of gray duct tape that was fastened across her mouth to drown out her screams. One of Van's cronies smiled as he placed the tape on tight. That motherfucker was going to be dead too.

I looked to Van. Just as he was about to put the cigar on a fresh patch of skin, I used every ounce of fight left inside me and was able to yank an arm free. That's all I needed. I stood up, but the chair was still chained to my legs. I just needed an arm. I grabbed Van's throat and squeezed as hard as I could. The life quickly drained from his face as his lips turned a shade of purple and then blue. I've killed many people, but none was going to feel as satisfying as this one. No one touched my girl and expected less of a punishment.

A hard crack across my back had me dropping to the ground, releasing Van's throat and sending his now unconscious body to the wet concrete. I turned to see the guy who had duct taped Sloan's mouth shut wielding a baseball bat. I stepped closer to him. My vision was black with rage. He swung the bat at me, but I caught his pathetic excuse of a swing with my free hand and ripped it from his grasp. I flipped the bat around in the air, catching the handle and swung once at his face. The sound of bone crunching filled the air between us. His jaw dislocated and shifted into an awkward angle as he collided with the concrete. I dropped the bat, turning to Sloan. She was hunched forward, her burn marks fiery red.

"Sloan, baby, look at me." I tilted her chin toward me, but her face was blank as she drifted into unconsciousness, likely due from the excruciating pain. Anger filled my veins once more, my blood running hot. I grabbed the bat from the floor as I made my way to Van. He, too, lay unconscious on the floor, his face no longer blue but slightly pink as the life was coming back to his face. While I lifted the bat, ready to end this man's life, Sloan spoke.

"Dean, where are you?" It was just a whisper, but I dropped the bat, racing to her side just as she was lifting her head.

"I'm here, right here."

Her eyes opened and locked on my face. Two more tears drifted down her perfect face. I kicked my chair out from behind me, so I could sit in front of her. I cupped her face with my free hand, and she rested her face into my palm.

"That hurt so bad." Her cries were just loud enough for me to hear. I leaned forward, resting my forehead to hers.

"I know, baby girl, I know. It's done now."

Her body twitched as she allowed herself to cry. We sat there for a moment longer than I felt comfortable, but she needed this embrace. She needed to know I was here and wasn't going anywhere.

"You're so strong." I kissed her tear-drenched lips, kissing away the wetness.

"I'm so sorry." I choked on my words as I held back the emotions bubbling in my chest.

CHAPTER 41

SLOAN

Dean was alive. He was here, and he'd saved me from anymore of Van's excruciating torture tactics. After he kissed me, Dean stood and made his way back to Van. He searched for the keys that still had him half attached to his chair. I leaned back in my chair as the sound of chains hit the concrete, and I saw Dean had successfully found the key and set himself free.

"Let's get you out of here." Dean made his way over to the back of my chair and began untying my ropes. As the first rope eased from my arm, I lifted it up and held my arm to my chest. I was sporting a few new burn marks that would inevitably scar. Turning to look at Dean's shirtless chest, I saw the burns all across his chest, each one red and angry with inflammation.

He made quick work of my remaining ropes, and

as soon as the last one fell to the ground, I was in his arms, my body trembling in his grasp.

"Oh my gosh! I'm so sorry. I didn't mean to hurt you." I pulled from his chest, realizing his burns were, no doubt, throbbing with pain.

My body lying against them was doing nothing for the pain. He didn't care, though. He pulled me back into his embrace, squeezing me tight. His head lay in the crook of my neck, inhaling my scent.

"I couldn't bear seeing you in that much pain. I'm so fucking sorry." His tone was deep and angry as he pulled me closer. Before I could reply, a faint groan caught my attention, and I turned to see Van, now conscious and rolling to his side on the floor. The growl that escaped Dean's mouth was wicked and evil. He dropped his arms from our embrace and walked over to pick up the metal bat from the floor. Gripping the bat in his hands, he stomped through the small amount of water, toward Van. With his heavy boot, he pushed Van's body over so that he was now lying on his back.

Van didn't say anything. He knew he'd fucked up, and if dying from a baseball bat was the way to go, he should consider himself lucky. I could have thought of more painful ways to die. Dean lifted the bat, above his head ready to strike.

"Wrong move, Dean." A voice echoed through the warehouse followed by the familiar crack of a bullet piercing the air around us. Blood sprayed from Dean's abdomen. He'd been shot.

CHAPTER 42

SLOAN

I couldn't remember having a day as shitty as this one, but this one definitely took the cake for the worst day of my life. Dean dropped the bat. The sound of metal bouncing off concrete caused my ears to ring. Running to Dean's side, I was able to catch his body before it hit the ground. Well, I was able to slow him from hitting the ground. His massive frame was too much for me, and I was not strong enough to hold him upright. We both fell to the floor, his body covering my legs.

"Dean! Dean! Stay with me!" I placed my hand over his abdomen, just left of his navel where his bullet wound now oozed blood, coating my hands. I pressed hard, trying to stop the bleeding, but the amount of blood that seeped through my fingers indicated I was not doing a good job of it.

"Dean, look at me, baby, look at me. Keep your eyes open. Can you do that for me?" He

stared into my eyes as his blinks started becoming more prolonged.

"Don't leave me, Dean. Don't you fucking leave me." I sobbed, holding his body to mine as I slowly watched the life drain from his face.

"Baby girl, you are so beautiful." His voice was a soft moan as his eyes stayed shut longer and longer.

"Don't do that, Dean! Keep your eyes on me!" I screamed, shaking his body. I needed to do something fast. If not, Dean was going to die right here. I needed to keep him talking, and I needed to keep him awake.

"What's your favorite sex position, Dean?" It was the first thing I could think of on the spot. His low chuckle meant it was the right question to ask. He coughed a few times, wincing through the pain before he answered.

"Any position where my dick is deep inside you." My lips lifted to a smile, but the way he opened his eyes, passion, lust, and something else danced across his face as his lips curled into the smallest of smiles. I leaned down and kissed his lips, showing him exactly how much I cared for him.

A set of footsteps echoed in the air. I looked up in panic, initially not seeing the culprit. My eyes scanned the room aggressively as fear started attacking me once again. In the corner of my eye, I caught the faint silhouette of a person standing in the shadows.

He stood there in the darkness, not allowing me to see who it was. I turned and noticed Van was now nowhere to be seen.

"Van, leave us the fuck alone!"

A devilish laugh echoed toward me, but the voice that responded was not Van's.

"It's over, Sloan. You never belonged to them. You were mine from the start. Now it's time to come with me. I'll try to make this as painless as possible."

Just then the ground vibrated beneath us, and the sound of glass shattering blew through the air. The explosion was so loud that every window in the building was blown inward. I lay my body on top of Dean's, protecting him from any debris that reached us. His eyes were closed, his lifeless body lay across my legs, and his face was emotionless against my chest.

The sound of bullets quickly entered the warehouse, but I just stayed where I was, lying across Dean, the man who had brought me back to life, as his now was slowly slipping from his body. I sobbed against his chest, blood pooling across his torso. I couldn't stop the blood. If he died, then I would die with him.

Everything fell silent—no more bullets, no more explosions, and the sound of nothingness filled my ears.

"She's right here. We need an ambulance now; there's a lot of blood." A familiar voice echoed beside me, but before I was able to see who it was, a sharp stab of a needle dug into my neck. I was gone once more. Darkness filled my body, my soul, and at this moment I realized the devil enjoyed my company a little too much. I slipped into the shadows of unconsciousness. The darkness, the place I had become all too familiar with. Son of a bitch. I'd been drugged. Again.

SNEAK PEEK

A Sneak Peek to
The Abyss
The sequel to The Shadows

CHAPTER 1

SLOAN

I've never been scared of the dark. It's my safe place, the place I can't be seen; therefore, no one can hurt me. Or so I thought. Darkness, to me, is something tangible. I can feel it in my hands, in my core, in my mind. It's a thick, inky black liquid that finds its way into even the smallest of crevices until you're so full it has nowhere else to go. You are no longer in the darkness; you've become the darkness.

I've always embraced the darkness, rather than fearing it. However, it wasn't until I could no longer see Dean's lifeless body beneath me that I tried to fight off the darkness that was quickly pulling me under. Fuck.

My head was pounding, and there was a slight ringing in my left ear that was annoying the fuck out of me. When I opened my eyes, I couldn't focus on anything.

My vision was so blurry I found myself blinking over and over to try and regain my eyesight. I was lying down, pushing myself up to a sitting position. I rubbed my eyes with the palms of my hands. Once I was able to see my surroundings, I found that I was alone. I was alone in what looked to be a hospital room, but not exactly. Everything was white. The walls, the door, the bed that I was sitting on. I swung my legs over the side of the bed. I felt a tug in the crook of my right arm. Looking down, I saw an IV was inserted, and I followed the line that was attached to a bag of clear fluids. Reading the bag, I saw that the contents of the bag read saline.

Where the actual fuck was I? And where was Dean? I looked across the room and saw there was a small table that contained bandages, tape, scissors, and more bags of fluid. Taking a few deep breaths, I looked down at my body and saw that I was now in a pair of sweatpants and a loose white t-shirt. Someone dressed me? As my breathing started to speed up, I felt scraping underneath my shirt. Pulling it up, I saw a bandage was covering each cigar burn I had been given. I was definitely in the hospital, wasn't I?

I stood from the bed and ripped the IV line from my arm, eager to leave and try to find Dean. The room was fairly small, so it only took me three long strides to get to the door. Grabbing the handle, I twisted the knob and swung the door open. Panic instantly swept over my body as my eyes locked on a man in all black, with a black ski mask pulled down covering his face. I screamed. Stepping back into the room, I started swinging my arms trying to defend myself.

"Owwie, owwie, sweetheart, it's me; it's Colson." He pulled his mask off, revealing his gorgeous face. He looked like he hadn't slept in days. He had dark rings under his eyes and the making of a bruise on his left cheek bone. The purplish color deepened into a black mass of pooled blood underneath his skin. He closed the gap between us and wrapped his arms around me so tight that I had to release the breath in my lungs.

I was breathing so fast that I thought I might faint, but the moment Colson's arms encased my body I collapsed in his arms. My eyes were burning with unshed tears, and I could no longer hold them back. I sobbed into his chest as we both fell to the ground. He held me in his lap for a long moment, letting me release all the emotions I had held while at the warehouse. He just sat there with me, whispering reassurances in my ear and I sobbed.

"Where are we? How did you find me? Where is Dean?" I had so many questions. I pushed off his chest, meeting his tired eyes. "Where is Dean? Is he okay?" He didn't answer me right away. He just stared into my eyes and pushed a loose strand of my hair behind my ear. Had he died in the warehouse? It was in that moment, that moment of possibly losing

Dean, that I began to realize how much these guys meant to me.

To be continued in

The Abyss
Book two in
The Darkness Trilogy

ACKNOWLEDGMENTS

To the readers, I thank you from the bottom of my heart, without you this book would merely be a paperweight.

To my incredible editor, Rosanna, I could never have made it here without you. Your knowledge and input enhanced this story to its full potential. I am so thankful for you.

To my amazing designer, Abigail, you brought my idea to fruition and truly made this cover more than I could have hoped for.

The Shadows was an idea of mine that came to me in a dream. Since I was little, I have allows had very vivid dreams. I was encouraged by my aunt to keep a journal of my dreams so I could reference back to them in the future.

This piece of advice would soon help me to write The Shadows, which took me roughly eight months to write. I have always enjoyed writing, but never in my wildest dreams did I think I would ever publish a piece of my work. Following my dream was the best decision of my career.

xoxo Rebecca Hamby

Printed in the USA
CPSIA information can be obtained
at www.ICGtesting.com
LVHW010747221223
767112LV00087B/3732

9 781088 002728